T0365636

DOUBLE IDENTITY

DOUBLE IDENTITY

Walter Norman Clark

iUniverse, Inc.
Bloomington

Double Identity

iUniverse books may be ordered through booksellers or by contacting:

iUniverse
1663 Liberty Drive
Bloomington, IN 47403
www.iuniverse.com
1-800-Authors (1-800-288-4677)

ISBN: 978-1-4759-3710-7 (sc)
ISBN: 978-1-4759-3711-4 (ebk)

Library of Congress Control Number: 2012912194

Printed in the United States of America

iUniverse rev. date: 02/19/2013

PROLOGUE

THE CHANGE

The rays of the rising 1918 October sun, after passing over a normal Germany terrain, and a French terrain that was battle scarred by four years of war passed through a window and over one of the many patients who was beginning to move as consciousness returned to his mind by degrees. From complete blackness, he was first aware that he was, that he was someone aware of his physical presence. There was pain in his head. He realized that he was lying down on his back on a bed. He could move his arms and legs. He slowly lifted his hands to where the searing pain in his head was. Moving his fingers over the throbbing part of his head they encountered bandages that seemed to swath the entire upper portion of his head, while leaving his nose, ears, eyes, mouth, and chin uncovered.

Again for a long time he lay motionless, trying to understand his situation. Why was he here, wherever here was? Then alarmingly the thought hit him, sending the other questions bolting into the background of his consciousness. He couldn't remember the past. Who was he? He couldn't even remember who he was! He could think. He knew he was in pain. He knew words, because in his mind he was talking to himself. He could ask himself questions. But he couldn't answer who he was.

Then, over his despairing thoughts, he began to hear something: a murmur of voices. Rising up on his elbows and turning his head, he saw a woman, dressed in white. A nurse. He was in a hospital. Apparently she was talking to patients in beds. At first he couldn't distinguish words, but as she came closer he could. When she got to his bed, she said, seemingly with a slight tremor in her voice, "Ah, Lieutenant Lessing, you have joined us. We'll get you some breakfast."

As she paused, he struggled with the words, finally whispering hoarsely, "You called me Lieutenant Lessing. Do you know who I am? Where am I? What has happened to me?"

He didn't realize the significance because he was under severe physical and emotional strain, and because the transition had happened so naturally, he hadn't even detected it. He had been thinking to himself in the English language, but when he heard the nurse's and the mens' voices, and when he then spoke to her, all the words-theirs, his, including those now in his thoughts-were in German; those in his thoughts were in perfect, unaccented German.

CHAPTER ONE

CHERBOURG, FRANCE
TWENTY-TWO YEARS LATER,
JUNE 17–18, 1940

As darkness descended on the dock at the harbor of Portsmouth on the southeast coast of England on June 17, 1940, the last dozen or so soldiers who had been rescued from the German army–dominated French coast disembarked from an ancient tugboat that had carried them to safety across the English Channel, to the harbor's dock. The captain of the boat was surprised to see that the evacuees were being replaced by a group of battle-prepared soldiers. The captain and Lieutenant Jacob W. L. Rosenstein, along with twelve privates and a sergeant, had been ordered to recross the channel to Cherbourg Harbor and pick up two tanks and several trucks along with their crews. Rosenstein's orders were to protect, if necessary, the tanks' crews, who were fighting a retreating action, and to help them load their equipment aboard the boat. The orders stipulated that the crews were his first priority, because they had learned much about the German army's tactics while fighting a rear-guard action as the British forces retreated south out of Belgium into France.

As the tugboat arrived at the Cherbourg Harbor entrance just before dawn, Rosenstein found the group waiting on the harbor's first wharf. As it was tied up to the wharf, Rosenstein could hear the rumble of tanks, which apparently had waited until dawn for their final attack. He quickly jumped off the boat and gestured his men, with their anti-tank weapons, into the wharf's deserted warehouses. The crew that was to be rescued, having aligned the equipment properly, within minutes were casting off the tug's tie lines, freeing the vessel for its quick exodus from the harbor.

Lieutenant Rosenstein, seeing the vessel's safe retreat, obeyed his orders, which were to surrender rather than die if the basic purpose of his mission—the safe departure of the crew and their equipment—was accomplished. He exited the warehouse with his hands in the air. Knowing the futility of fighting the overwhelming enemy force, he gestured to his men to do the same. The German tank commander, while cursing their failure to stop the boat, accepted the British lieutenant's surrender. Stripped of everything but the clothes on their backs, the captured soldiers spent most of the day sitting on the wharf, overseen by groups of German soldiers.

In the late afternoon they were ordered to their feet and escorted to the town hall, their pace quickening at the promise of food. As they trudged down Boulevard Felix Amoit, the lieutenant was accosted by a German Unteroffizier, or sergeant, who pulled him aside and into the main room of an inn. Inside, the soldier led him to a small table and pushed him down into one of its two chairs, with the command "sit." The German then walked over to another small table. Rosenstein looked around. Other than himself and the Unteroffizier, the room was empty except for two privates standing by the door. He noticed that there were two interior doors entering the room: one open, the other closed. From the open door came a sound like someone snoring.

Before he could contemplate what that meant, the other door burst open and a rather small German major strutted through it and over to the other chair, plopping down onto it as he said in rather good but stilted English, "All right, let's begin. What is your name and …"

CHAPTER TWO

CHERBOURG, FRANCE

JUNE 18, 1940

Oberst Wilhelm Lessing was sitting wearily on a chair in the front bedroom of the German army's requisitioned inn on Boulevard Felix Amoit near the waterfront in Cherbourg, France. Lessing, from Admiral Wilhelm Canaris's Abwehr, the German foreign intelligence group, selected because of his fluency in English and French, had been following the advance of the German army's blitzkrieg through Belgium and France. He had been questioning captured British, French, and Polish soldiers for more than three weeks. The objective was to gather information about the strength, both in numbers and armaments, of the enemy units that were retreating. He thought that continuing the questioning now seemed to be a wasted effort. The British and French were finished.

From the beaches of the North Sea at Dunkirk, France, where most of the remnants of the British Expeditionary Force and units of the French army had, two weeks earlier, scrambled onto boats to save themselves from the overwhelming advance of Germany's panzer divisions; from Calais, where more escaped; from Saint Valery-en-Caux, Saint Malo, Le Harve, and now here at Cherbourg, the story was the same.

Although, he thought, perhaps as many as a hundred thousand might have escaped by boat to England with few if any weapons, they were defeated and no longer a threat to the army. Germany had conquered all of Western Europe. Lessing was beginning to believe that the war was as good as over. Soon he would be back at Abwehr headquarters in Hamburg.

Lessing was in his midforties. He had been promoted from lieutenant colonel to Oberst (German for "colonel"), which probably was the appropriate rank for this assignment. His six-foot, 180-pound, muscular body was topped by what had at one time probably been a handsome, strong-featured, slightly elongated, blue-eyed face on a head covered with receding black hair. His face was blotched by a faint, broad, three-inch diagonal scar from an old wound just below his hairline. He had another scar that was hidden by a small black mustache. Although it distracted from what probably would otherwise still have been considered handsome good looks, the scar oddly made his face more interesting, distinguishing it from the bland, blond-haired poster faces of Hitler's ideal of the master race.

He was wearing a neatly tailored uniform, whose only decoration other than his rank insignia and the stripes signifying that he had been wounded in the First World War was a small pin, representing the war's Knights Cross. His travel valise was sitting on another chair. His holster, with a Lugar pistol in it, was draped over the chair's back. His visor cap lay on a shelf alongside a stack of books belonging to the inn's French owner.

Lessing, who spoke perfect French, had been amused when in his sparse French, Major Manz, Lessing's second in command, had dispossessed the owner of the inn. Manz had allowed him, his family, and the inn's guests half an hour to collect their belongings and leave, with the vague promise that there would be proper compensation to the inn's owner at some time in the future. With only a slight tug at his conscience, Lessing neither knew nor cared where they had gone.

Deciding there was probably nothing more of importance to be gleaned from questioning the remaining prisoners, he had left the task of interrogating these last remnants of the British Expeditionary Force to Manz.

The latest prisoner was a young British lieutenant, captured with a few enlisted men on the Cherbourg Harbor docks. The German troops who had captured them had missed capturing a small ship that had left the dock just minutes before the British contingent had surrendered.

Lessing only half-listened to the interrogation, in English, going on in the adjacent front room of the inn. He was thinking that perhaps, with the action slowing down from the last couple of hectic fortnights, he could find a decent restaurant in this French town and have the chef give him a proper sit-down meal with a good French wine.

Manz was asking the routine questions in his slightly accented upper-class, British-timbred voice. Manz was not a member of Canaris's Abwehr. A member of the Schutzstaffel, or SS, he was "on loan" from Heinrich Himmler's Gestapo—"on loan" being the result of a "request" from Hitler. Canaris and Himmler secretly hated each other, but with Hitler looking on, they gave the surface appearance of cooperation. It was quite possible that reinforcing Lessing's promotion was Canaris's need to make sure his man was in charge. Although Lessing, as was the case with most Abwehr officers, had no fondness for members of the SS, he was quite satisfied with Manz's assistance in their assignment.

"What is your name and rank? What was your unit? Who are your commanding officers? Which of them have escaped? What have been the losses of your unit? How many other men of your unit do you think escaped at the harbor? What armaments and equipment did they take with them?" Apparently Manz was unaware that the prisoner was not caught escaping, but helping escapees.

The British soldier (considering the adverse circumstances of his present situation) replied in a surprisingly strong, clear English voice, "Lieutenant Jacob W. L. Rosenstein. That is all I am prepared to say."

Only half-hearing the answer, Lessing was suddenly jerked out of his reverie. What had the man said? Where had he heard that name before? Where had he heard that voice before?

He rose from his chair and went to the door connecting the two rooms. The British lieutenant was sitting at a small table in the sparsely furnished room, facing toward the door where Lessing was standing. Manz was sitting in another chair across the table from the prisoner, his back to Lessing. Sitting at what appeared to be a dining table, a sergeant was taking notes on a pad in a hard-backed folder. Just inside the front door, two helmeted soldiers stood, half-lounging on their rifles, not understanding a word of the English conversation and bored by the oft-repeated verbal exercise going on inside the room. Outside on the narrow Boulevard Felix Amiot, in the deepening dusk dampened by a light summer rain, trucks rumbled by, carrying supplies to the panzer division that was completing the capture of the Cherbourg Peninsula. A captured train on the railroad track on the other side of the boulevard was slowing down as it approached the town center.

Lessing stared at the British soldier. His uniform, although soiled and wrinkled, was properly buttoned and, despite its present condition, seemed to fit him perfectly. Even though he was sitting down, it was easy to see that he was a tall, muscular man, appearing too youthful to be an officer, seemingly hardly out of his teens. His face—handsome, strong-featured, intense, blue-eyed, slightly elongated, and topped with straight, combed-back black hair—was, in Lessing's eyes, surprisingly familiar.

Manz, hearing the sound of Lessing's movements, jerked his head around toward the door and asked in German, "Is something wrong, Oberst?"

In perfect, unaccented English, Lessing replied pleasantly, "I am just interested in the lieutenant's name. A double middle initial—a bit unusual, even for an Englishman. Tell me, Lieutenant, what do the W and L stand for?" The Englishman, starring at Lessing with a slightly puzzled frown appearing on his face, hesitated.

"Come on, Lieutenant," continued Lessing. "I know it's not the best of times for you. But the Geneva Convention does allow us to get you to tell us your name. That can't be a military secret. Even under these circumstances, there is no reason why we can't on this simple matter be civil with each other."

Shrugging, Rosenstein replied, "William Lessing. It was my father's name."

Shocked by the name Lessing, Lessing struggled to regain control. "Your father's? If so, why do you have the surname Rosenstein?"

The Englishman, the puzzled expression on his face deepening, waited a full minute before replying, just as Manz started to rebuke him. "My father was lost in the last month of the last war, shortly after I was born. My mother, Penny Lessing, died in childbirth as the result of an accident. My father's sister, my aunt Martha, and her husband, Jacob Rosenstein, adopted me, giving me his first name and surname, with my father's names as middle names."

On hearing the answer, Lessing gave an involuntary gasp, not knowing why he did so. Manz, who had turned his head back toward the Englishman when he had spoken, stared at him for a moment, apparently not hearing Lessing's gasp. He then turned back toward the Oberst with a surprised expression, saying in German, "What a remarkable coincidence, Oberst. That is the English version of your name." He then turned around back to the prisoner, adding, "And I must say he bears somewhat of a resemblance to you. Could this man be related to you?"

Lessing, while still struggling in his mind to remember something, quickly recovered outwardly from his astonishment and casually replied, also in German, "It's possible, I suppose, although I don't know of any English relatives that I may have. However, there are many German/English relationships. The kaiser, poor wretched soul that he is, is even related to the king of England—or is it his wife?—in some way."

He paused, trying but failing to bring something that the conversation had seemed to trigger in his memory to the forefront of his mind. With the eyes of the five men staring at him, he finally spoke, drowning out the beginning of another question by Manz. "I don't think this man has anything to tell us that will be useful.

Send him back with the other prisoners and let's go get something to eat."

When Lessing had come to the doorway, the two soldiers had quickly come to attention, and as the words turned to understood German from English, they suddenly showed more interest in what was being said. The sergeant looked up from his pad, also following the exchanges with interest. During the silence of the pause in their commander's conversation, the three exchanged puzzled glances.

As Lessing turned to go back into the bedroom to get his holster and cap, he heard Manz issue a command to the sergeant. "Make a note of the prisoner's full name, Jacob William Lessing Rosenstein." He placed an added emphasis when saying the last name. "And be sure to place a check after the name, as you have been instructed to do with similar names, and then we'll take him to the town hall and lock him up with the other prisoners."

The sergeant, after making some notations on his pad, now also noticed the resemblance between the prisoner and his commanding officer. With some respect in his voice, he said to the Englishman in heavily accented English, "Stand up and follow me."

With one last puzzled glance at Lessing, he did so, followed by the two soldiers out through the building's front door.

As Lessing prepared to go out, he mulled over in his mind the puzzle of similar names. Was it possible he had English relatives? After all, he had no memory of the first half of his life.

Lessing and Manz had dinner together at a nearby restaurant, prepared by the restaurant owner himself. As they ate, the only reference Lessing made to their task was asking Manz if the prisoners they had been interrogating were still being held in the town hall or had been sent to the prisoner-holding facility. Manz told him that those they had been interrogating for the past few days were being held temporarily, under heavy guard, in the town hall, until a train arrived to take them to a prisoner-of-war camp. Weary of the questioning procedure, which had been going on for well over a fortnight, sixteen or more hours a day, they retired to their rooms in the inn.

CHAPTER THREE

CHERBOURG, FRANCE

JUNE 18, 1940

That night Lessing lay in the Frenchman's bed (remade by the inn's maid, commandeered by Manz) trying to sleep. He couldn't get the vision of the British officer out of his mind. He was certain that he had seen him, or at least someone like him, somewhere, but he couldn't recall where. And the name Rosenstein also seemed to strike a chord in his memory. And the middle names! The same as his! Perhaps that was the reason for these vague remembrances—just the coincidence of the similarity in names.

Before the war, his work with the Abwehr counterintelligence section from time to time had involved him with English officers. One of the reasons Canaris had chosen him for his service was his excellent command of English, Portuguese, French, and Spanish. However, he had seldom been involved with junior officers. He was certain that if he had dealt with someone with the name of Rosenstein, a rather peculiar name for an Englishman, especially one with the middle initials W. L., he would have remembered it.

His thoughts about Canaris selecting him for his intelligence team in the winter of 1936 because of his grasp of languages sent his thoughts back further in time to when he discovered that he could speak both English and French. That in turn swept his mind back to the hospital in late 1918. He was continually haunted by the fact that he could remember nothing about his life before he regained consciousness in that field hospital more than two decades earlier. Perhaps he did have relatives who were English. He just couldn't remember them!

He had learned that the matron's name was Hilga Regensburg from the soldier in the next bed. In answer to his questions, she told him that he was in a military field hospital several kilometers behind the front lines. He had been found unconscious in a group of shell-battered houses a few hundred meters behind the trenches.

His uniform had been badly damaged by a shell's explosion. Any identification papers he might have had were assumed to have been lost in the confusion when he was discovered unconscious some time after the British shelling had ceased. The only identification he had had was the Oberleutenant insignia on his tattered uniform and his name etched on the back of a Knights Cross, Germany's highest medal of valor, that had been attached to a cord around his neck. He had no memory of why he had been awarded the medal. His helmet was badly dented on the left side, apparently hit by a fragment of the shell. Although the helmet had probably saved his life, the fragment had hit with such force that he had been badly concussed. The bodies of several soldiers were near his, apparently victims of the same shell that had wounded him.

At the time there had been great confusion caused by a vicious shelling, followed by a battalion-sized attack on their lines by the British forces. It had finally been repulsed, with heavy casualties on both sides. With the resulting overload of wounded and the further confusion of the armistice, officially bringing about Germany's defeat about a fortnight later, the hospital staff hadn't made any great effort to find his unit.

He had been unconscious for two days after he was brought to the hospital with the two severe head wounds, one on the front as well as one on the left side. The latter had probably caused his head to concuss, which led to his intense head pain. Additionally, a shell fragment had creased his upper lip. He apparently had turned his head when the shell exploded, with one fragment hitting him broadside on the left side of his head and two other passing fragments causing the wounds on his face.

He had no memory at all of his life before he regained consciousness in the hospital. The doctor at the field hospital who had treated him said that such loss of memory, post-trauma amnesia, was not too unusual after a severe head wound. Additionally, the shock of battle also often caused temporary amnesia. However, in his case the amnesia was not temporary. He had never had any memories of his life before being wounded.

In early December, within a month after the end of the war, he and the other wounded were removed from the field hospital in France, joining the hundreds of thousands of defeated but still orderly German soldiers as they marched through the rain and mud for the journey of more than 200 miles to the Rhine River and home in Germany.

They had bypassed the shattered Belgian and French villages and towns, hoping to avoid the curses and thrown stones or perhaps worse actions of their inhabitants. Seeing the devastated countryside—rutted, gouged, and cratered like a moonscape—that the years of war had bequeathed to northern France and Belgium, they could well imagine the anger these people felt toward them, the defeated Huns. Hot on their heels a scant few miles to their rear, they were followed by the victorious Allied armies. They traveled through the ravaged French and Belgian lands, usually at night, again hoping to avoid contact, even in the countryside, with the victorious but still hostile inhabitants of the region. Still disciplined soldiers, they sanitarily buried their wastes.

The hospital staff, with Lessing and the other walking wounded, had joined them. They trudged along with a group of the defeated soldiers, the wounded who were unable to walk carried in carts pulled by soldiers. Because there hadn't been time to bury them in the burial ground adjacent to the hospital, the bodies of their wounded comrades who had died just before the hospital had been shut down were also carried on the carts. As they neared their homeland, they quickened their pace, covering as much as twenty-five miles a day.

When they neared the Rhine River, they found a Germany largely physically unscathed by the war. Having continued carrying the bodies of their fallen comrades, including those who had died during the march, they buried them in a cemetery just outside the medieval walls of a small town. Laid in a row against the back stone wall of the burial ground, their graves were marked by headstones, each bearing a common date of death—November 11, 1918—and, when it was known, the deceased's name and rank.

The hospital staff and the wounded arrived at a permanent hospital in the Rhineland near the small city of Bonn, the birthplace of Ludwig von Beethoven, the famous German composer. There, Lessing found that his wounds, which at first the doctor had thought were serious, were not, because other than the amnesia, they had healed rather quickly. Because of the influx of wounded and the further confusion of the armistice, the overworked doctors had been unable to properly graft skin to what was essentially a large flesh wound on his forehead. The healing of the wound therefore left a broad, diagonal, three-inch-long scar on his forehead. The wound to the side of his head had also left a scar, although not as large, and when he let his hair grow longer, it was soon almost completely unnoticeable.

By the time he was officially discharged from the hospital, the war had been over for more than a month. In the confusion, he was never found by his military unit. In his state of mind at the time, he had no prior memory, so he didn't know what, where, or whom to look for. He was soon just one of millions of ex-soldiers of a defeated army heading for home and their families. However, with no memory, he didn't know either where "home" was or who "family" was. Not knowing where to go, and feeling that he needed time to assess his situation, he asked the hospital's head doctor if he could stay—not as a patient, but as an orderly, with a bed in the orderly dormitory and food from the hospital kitchen as his pay. The doctor agreed.

During Lessing's stay at the hospital, he developed a friendship with one of the younger doctors, Hans Brachman. During evenings in the doctor's sparse quarters, they would discuss his memory problem. Brachman said the temporary loss of memory after a severe trauma such as the shrapnel wounds to the side of his head and forehead often resulted in post-trauma amnesia. However, in the overwhelming number of cases, such loss of memory was only temporary, and within days or at most a week or two, most if not all memory would return.

But even though Lessing retained learned skills, he still had no memories of his personal life. He obviously had had a good education. His spoken and written grammar were perfect. He discovered that he had additional language skills. He had understood perfectly the officious French officer speaking to the French soldiers who had overseen their summary departure from France. Not only could he read and write with proficiency, but as he looked through Brachman's meager but surprisingly comprehensive book collection, he found that he comprehended advanced mathematics and other sciences. And during this browsing through the library shelves hoping to find something that would explain his continued amnesia, he had come across some of Freud's papers—oddly enough, copies written in English—and found that he was also skilled in English. In spite of his amnesia, he had known what Freud's field was and had eagerly read the papers, hoping to get some insight into his problem, to no avail.

Brachman said this seemingly diametric, perfect memory of learned skills coupled with complete loss of personal memory was unknown in his experience. However, he said, perhaps there was an explanation. Maybe when someone suffered a tragic personal trauma, the subconscious mind looked for an excuse to wipe out the memory, perhaps by hiding it in the deepest recesses of the mind. Perhaps in Lessing's case the head wound was the perfect excuse for his subconscious to excise some personal tragic memory and, along with it, all other personal memory that might bring back the unbearable, unwanted tragic remembrances. Whatever the reason, his remembrance of events before he had woken up in the field hospital had not returned.

Former Oberleutenant, now Herr, Wilhelm Lessing was no longer a soldier but an unemployed civilian, as were millions of his fellow countrymen, when he left the hospital for good in February 1919. As Oberst Lessing recalled these events that had happened more than twenty years earlier, for seemingly the thousandth time, he finally drifted into a dreamless sleep.

CHAPTER FOUR

WILHELM LESSING'S LIFE
1918–1940

After leaving the hospital in early February 1919, the former Lieutenant Lessing, not knowing where home was in Germany, had been offered a teaching position in Zurich, Switzerland, and left Germany. While in the hospital, he had met a high ranking official from the Swiss Red Cross, Heinrich Fuerst, who was acquainted with Hans Brachman. Fuerst, forty years old, was a Swiss man whose mother was German, as was his wife. He owned an armaments factory near Zurich. Switzerland was supposed to be neutral, but because he was a German-speaking Swiss, his sympathies lay with the country just over the border to the north. He had grown rich, supplying the kaiser's armies both before and during the war with armaments and munitions. By shipping through Trieste via Portuguese ships to Stockholm, the delusion of neutrality was maintained. From Stockholm the shipments were reloaded onto German ships and went thence to Germany. He had salved his conscience of being in the business of manufacturing instruments of destruction by becoming an active member of the Red Cross. That December in 1918 he was in Germany determining the needs of the defeated country's hospitals for the war wounded.

He had met Lessing one evening when Lessing was in Brachman's room, immersed in the writings of Freud. Fuerst was surprised that Lessing, a lowly hospital orderly, was by himself in a doctor's room and that he was reading a scientific paper in English.

While waiting for Brachman to join him, he had engaged Lessing in conversation. He became most interested in Lessing's lack of memories of his life before being wounded. He asked probing questions, trying to unlock the younger man's memory, to no avail. During the lengthy conversation, he became aware of how well educated Lessing appeared to be as he steered the conversation to other matters. After about half an hour, Fuerst abruptly switched to English, having noticed that the paper Lessing had been reading was written in that language. Lessing answered back fluently in the same tongue, cracking a small smile as he did so. A while later Fuerst switched to Portuguese, having learned the rudiments of the language because of his shipping needs, with the same surprising result.

Fuerst was amazed that although the bewildered young man had memories of general things that had happened during the years of his young life, he could not relate personally to them. He knew that he had been to school, including university, but he couldn't remember where, or who his teachers and schoolmates were. He felt that he had had a normal and happy childhood but couldn't recall any particulars. He knew that obviously, he had had a mother and father and perhaps brothers and sisters, but he couldn't visualize them in his mind.

Lessing knew that he was attracted to the young nurses on the hospital staff, especially Hilga, whom he had met on his first day. However, he had no recollection of any relations with other women before that day. He had not been wearing a wedding ring, so he probably wasn't married, but perhaps he was. He just didn't know. As he was a lieutenant, he knew he must have been in the army for some time, but he couldn't remember any particulars of his army life, other than military skills, before waking up in the field hospital. He was continually finding out that he had a rather broad comprehensive knowledge of science and history. But he had no remembrances whatever of how he fit into the latter. It was as if on that fateful late October day, a steel gate had slammed shut over a portion of Lessing's brain, shutting out his personal history from the present. And he couldn't find the key to open it.

Fuerst's thirteen-year-old son, Julian, was attending a private, exclusive school for teenage boys in Zurich. His father had become aware of Lessing's multiple language skills and his knowledge of other subjects. And he was impressed that, even with his memory problem, the young man quickly became friendly with the people around him. With the favorable personal impression that he made, Fuerst thought Lessing could fill a vacant position of language instructor at his son's school. Weighing heavily in the decision was the fact that Lessing's lack of memory probably meant that he would have no prejudgments about teenage boys' behavior. The younger man's toned, well-muscled body was also a plus in dealing with teenage boys. Herr Fuerst wanted someone he thought he could rely on to keep track of Julian's problem while his father was away from home. Herr Fuerst had told Lessing of Julian's problem. His mother, who was a German, had died when he was only five years old. Fuerst's business requirements required long days at the factory as well as frequent out-of-town trips. This, he said, left him little time for the upbringing of a small child. For the next few years there was a series of nannies; none of whom, in spite of generous remuneration from Fuerst, lasted for more than a few months. For Julian had quickly developed into a problem child. He was unruly and disobedient. Probably in an attempt to get attention, he developed a tendency to throw and destroy his toys. Of which his father gave him an ample supply. Replacing those as needed with little admonition. As he grew older the throwing and destroying expanded into more serious objects, including small animals. When he was nine his father enrolled him in a school for boys. By thirteen he was going to the Zurich Exclusive Gymnasium for Boys

So in early February he accompanied Lessing, who had quickly said yes, to the immigration station at the Swiss border. He was outfitted in new clothes both on his body and in a new valise, all purchased by Fuerst. The border guards normally were very selective in admitting Germans into the country after the war. Fuerst, however, because of his position, knew where to pull the necessary strings to bypass policy, and the imaginary line was crossed with no difficulty.

As an applicant lacking any history about his educational background, Lessing normally wouldn't have gotten past the massive oaken front door of the rather forbidding-looking, gray-stone, four-story building that housed the school. Again, however, accompanied by Herr Fuerst, an elderly doorman ushered them into the office of the headmaster without question. An hour later, the Zurich Exclusive Gymnasium for Boys had a new assistant tutor.

Although the pay wasn't much, the position included room and board, the latter of a much greater quantity and better quality than Lessing had been getting at the hospital. He was provided a small room, on the fifth floor of the building. The room was small and in a garret-type attic, but compared with the orderlies' dormitory at the hospital, it was sumptuous. It was heated by a hot-water radiator. There was a single bed, a table and two chairs, a bookcase, a wardrobe, and a washstand with a metal basin and pitcher. Everything was of good quality and in good condition. Hot and cold water were available down the hall, as was the necessity and a bathtub. He shared the latter with two other assistant tutors with quarters on the same floor.

Lessing soon learned that "exclusive" didn't just mean that the school's students were sons of wealthy fathers. They all were, of course. The tuition fees were such that only the wealthy could afford them. There were no scholarship students. Exclusive also meant that it accepted boys other schools wouldn't accept because of behavior problems. In addition to an excellent education program, there was strict discipline.

A rigorous two-fortnight course on student instruction by an assistant headmaster was sufficient to give Lessing the rudiments of how to teach teenage boys French, English, and German—German because not all the students were German-speaking Swiss. Given the appropriate textbooks, he and the headmaster were surprised at the ease with which he fit into the role of tutor. Being not too much older than his students, he soon developed a rapport with the teenage boys. As requested by his benefactor, Herr Fuerst, he made a special effort to seek out Julian Fuerst.

For the first few months Lessing was at the school, he experienced varying scenarios of the same basic dream almost every night, which also had been the case in the hospital. He was trying to find his way home. Sometimes he was in the downtown area of a large city, and other times he was in the countryside, walking or running the streets or roads or pathways, but invariably encountering various types of obstacles in trying to reach his destination.

In the city his objective was the fourth floor in a multistory building. The streets and buildings seemed familiar yet strange. In the countryside it wasn't a building that was the objective but a small town. In the countryside dreams, however, there didn't seem to be much familiarity in the terrain. City obstacles would be such mundane ones as missing a bus or catching the wrong one, or encountering a dead end to a street, or entering a building and being unable to find a way out, or simply getting lost. Sometimes the obstacles were more bizarre, such as encountering a torrent of water inexplicably rushing down a street, or suddenly facing a large building where none had been before. The result was always the same. He always woke up before reaching his destination. He never got home. The content of the various dreams set in the countryside was much simpler. He lost his way, he tried to get a ride but failed, or night would simply fall before he reached his destination. Strangely, all the street signs in all of the dreams were in French.

However, between spending long hours teaching, the school's sports programs (his well-muscled body helped), and studying himself, he found that he was beginning to cope with his amnesia. The dreams became less frequent until they occurred only every month or so. Perhaps the school was becoming his home and the other tutors and the boys were becoming his family.

Lessing was aware of happenings in Germany, such as the turmoil that was taking place in Berlin, where disgruntled sailors from the German fleet had taken over the Imperial Palace, and the many postwar problems elsewhere. However, for the next five years, problems in Germany were not a concern for him. After all, even though he was a German, he had no recollection of his life as a German before 1918 and had lived only three months as a German before entering Switzerland.

In 1924 Julian graduated with honors and went to work in his father's company. Life in the school had enabled him, with Lessing's help, to overcome his problems. At eighteen he was, in temperament, an adult. And he had become a close adult friend of Lessing, who was about nine years his senior.

A year later, in 1925, Lessing suddenly tired of his life as a teacher, perhaps because Julian was no longer there. He followed Julian into Fuerst's armaments company. With his wide knowledge of languages and the culture of other countries (how he had acquired them, he did not know), he became one of the company's foreign international salesmen. To achieve this position, he was given an intense schooling about the company's products, which were primarily small guns, such as pistols, rifles, and machine guns, and land mines.

Because Lessing was a German, Germany was his principal sales area. The Treaty of Versailles had allowed Germany to have an army of only 100,000 men, and by 1925 the Weimar government had recovered enough to fund over the next few years the purchase of enough armaments for the full army. Lessing was doing rather well as a civilian. However, the financial crash of 1929 suddenly dried up a large portion of Fuerst's market. During his selling days in Germany, Lessing had dealt primarily with Generalmajor Frederick Gompp, who was one of the youngest senior officers in the postwar army. By coincidence Gompp, in 1919, had been one of the wounded soldiers at the same hospital at the same time as Lessing. He had been one of the defeated, along with Lessing, who had marched back to Germany. He had stayed in the army, being one of the 100,000. Even though he was several years older, he and Lessing became friends.

Lessing, sensing that because he was the less senior salesperson, Fuerst quite possibly would reluctantly be laying him off, quit the company. He didn't really make a sacrifice, as Gompp had an open slot in his officers' group. So Lessing in July 1929 "rejoined" the German army. Even though there were no records of an Oberleutenant Lessing, Gompp had become impressed with Lessing's knowledge of military affairs, despite his amnesia problem. With Gompp's help, Lessing rejoined as a captain. The Weimar government was already secretly expanding the German army beyond the 100,000. With his experience working with teenagers at the school, he was assigned to supervise the training of recruits, most of whom were young men who were unable to find work because of the accelerating economic depression. For the next five years, Lessing was on the fringe of the expanding army, continuing in the training of recruits. In 1932 he advanced in rank to major. He stayed out of the politics involving Hitler's Brown Shirt Sturmabteilung, or SA. He was appalled at the massacre of more than one hundred officers and politicians on the last weekend of June 1934. And as an officer, he was required to take the following oath:

> I swear by God this sacred oath: I will render unconditional obedience to Adolf Hitler, the Führer of the German Reich and people, Supreme Commander of the Armed Forces, and will be ready as a brave soldier to risk my life at any time for this oath.

To Lessing this unprecedented oath to Hitler personally, not the German state or constitution, was not right. His experience with recruits, and in many cases their families, convinced him that his responsibility was to his country and its people, not solely to an individual. For some reason deep down in his amnesia-locked mind, he knew there could be circumstances in which he could not adhere to this oath. But what could he do? He had a good life in the army, with friends and other junior officers, and going back into civilian life didn't appeal to him. He probably wouldn't be allowed to resign anyway. Then in 1935, he was reprieved.

His friend and superior officer, Gompp, had joined Admiral Wilhelm Canaris when he took over command of the Abwehr, Germany's intelligence organization. The Abwehr was almost completely separated from the German army and its Nazi SS.

Gompp recommended to the admiral that he also take Lessing, because in addition to his many positive attributes, there was his command of several languages.

Lessing was assigned to the foreign branch, where he spent the first three years primarily translating and interpreting documents secured by other members of the organization. In 1938, he was advanced to the rank of lieutenant colonel and attached to Germany's embassy in Madrid. There he was acting as communications director, but his real job was keeping an eye on Canaris's "friend" Francisco Franco, a position he held even after the war started, until he was assigned the task of interrogating captured prisoners.

CHAPTER FIVE

CHERBOURG, FRANCE

JUNE 21, 1940

Once again consciousness returned to Lessing in degrees. From complete blackness, he was first aware that he was someone. Immediately the throbbing pain in his head hit him. For some time he was aware only of the pain, the overwhelming pain. Then it began to diminish a bit, or perhaps he was beginning to endure it.

Opening his eyes, he raised himself up on his elbows. Looking around, he realized he was lying on his back in a bed, one of six in a fairly large room. All the beds were covered with white sheets, and all but his were empty. When he saw that he was in a white hospital gown, he realized that he was in a hospital. Putting his left hand up to the side of his head where the pain seemed to be emanating from, he encountered a heavy bandage. He had been wounded. Closing his eyes, he mentally envisioned his last conscious recollection.

Shortly after the early October twilight, in the dark of an overcast sky, wearing the cleaned and mended, altered-to-fit uniform recovered from the body of a German Oberleutenant, he had crept across no-man's-land, past machine-gun nests manned by weary German soldiers who were all but defeated. The British unit manning that section of the line had started a firefight a few hundred yards to his left to divert the attention of the Germans from his advancement. In what was left of a small village several hundred yards from the front line, he had been approaching a small group of German soldiers crouched down around a small fire in front of a small shelled-out building.

He remembered that he thought he had seen the sleeve insignia of an Unteroffizier on one of them and thinking, *Good*. Chances were he would have the German defensive information that was needed for the attack planned for the early dawn hours later. As a superior to the Unteroffizier, he very likely could finagle it out of him. And the Knights Cross around his neck, also appropriated from the German Oberleutenant's body, would make the soldiers somewhat in awe of their superior officer.

As he approached them, he had yelled, "Hello! Where is the rest of your unit?"

As several figures turned toward him, half-rising, the rumble of an incoming shell caused him to instinctively throw himself to the ground. This probably had saved his life, because the last thing he remembered was the group around the fire disappearing in a blinding flash as he felt a searing pain in his head.

The pain was still there as he again opened his eyes and gazed around. He noticed a written notice on the wall beside the bed. Oddly, it was in French, which he spoke as well as German. To better read it, he leaned forward, his head passing by a mirror on the small chest beside the bed. He jerked his head back and looked directly into the mirror.

The face staring back at him was not him! Its most noticeable feature was a broad three-inch diagonal scar on what should have been an unscarred, as Penny had lovingly called it, "noble brow." And although on second glance, other than the scar, the face did look somewhat like his, it was older, the skin more weathered. There were little wrinkles around the eyes. The hair was not only longer but seemingly thinner, worn in a different style with a slight trace of gray at the temples. And the face had a light brown mustache!

The thought of Penny brought added pain to his throbbing head—not physical pain but mental anguish. The news of her death, at the very moment that the joy of their lives, the birth of their first child, was almost due, had almost driven him insane. It was why he had volunteered for this last excursion across the lines. He had hoped that the danger of the assignment would force the mental anguish out of his mind. Or perhaps his subconscious was hoping he would be killed, ending the torment. Before he could consciously assimilate both the memory of Penny's death and the shock of the disparity of his face and the image in the mirror, he heard someone entering the room. Turning his head toward the door, he saw a soldier standing by it. He had the collar insignia of a major in the German army, but his uniform was of a different cut and color from any that he had ever seen before. He was of medium height, with a rounded face and rather prominent ears. He was wearing steel-framed glasses, which partially obscured the size of his eyes.

The officer addressed Lessing in German. At least Lessing was pretty sure he was the one being addressed, since he was the only person in the room. "Ah, Oberst, I'm glad to see that you are awake. You had us worried. You have been unconscious for more than two days now, ever since the accident."

Lessing thought, *It's a German hospital, not French. I'll have to be alert—no English. But he addressed me as Oberst?*

Before he could think further, the major continued. "When the errant bomb accidentally dropped from the Stuka hit the inn, I was at the town hall arranging for the prisoners' transportation back to the fatherland. A train with its drivers had unexpectedly become available. I had been aroused from my bed by the Unteroffizier before I had hardly an hour's sleep. But I was fortunate, as the room I had been sleeping in was where the bomb hit, and it was completely demolished. Fortunately, it wasn't armed and didn't explode, or you would have been blown to bits. One of the ceiling beams in your room fell and grazed the side of your head, right where your old wound was. You have been unconscious ever since."

Lessing thought, *What is he talking about? What is a Stuka? What town hall? What prisoners? Old wound? Sleeping in a room?*

Before Lessing could blurt the questions aloud, his reaction, honed by experience as an agent, prevailed, and he closed his eyes and pretended to fall back into unconsciousness. He heard the German shout in alarm, "Matron, the Oberst is again unconscious! Come and bring Doctor Brachman!"

As Lessing heard the voices of a woman and a man added to that of the major, he kept his eyes closed and listened to what they were saying, hoping to get further information about his puzzling situation.

The voice of the man, also German, in a soothing tone that sounded vaguely familiar, now spoke. "Don't be alarmed, Major. It is not unusual with a head wound such as the Oberst has for the patient to slip out of and then back into unconsciousness. Wilhelm will probably come to again before too long. Meanwhile, we'll have to make plans for what to do with him. It depends on the seriousness of the wound. If it isn't too serious, we can keep him here at this French infirmary. But if it turns out to have caused extensive damage to his brain, then we'll have to get him back to a major hospital as quickly as possible."

The voice of the major replied, "How long will it be before you know? I'll have to keep Admiral Canaris informed. Fortunately, with the last of the defeated British forces having left France, our present assignment here is practically finished. I'll be at the town hall. Please inform me of his condition as soon as you can determine it. Heil Hitler!"

The voices of the doctor and the woman, presumably a nurse, both responded with a "Heil Hitler," that of the nurse with enthusiasm, that from the doctor seemingly with something less than enthusiasm in his tone.

The doctor continued, "As soon as he wakes up again, let me know."

As he spoke, the diminishing volume of his voice indicated they were leaving the room. In the quiet of the room, Lessing lay still, eyes still closed, trying to unravel what he had heard. In addition to Stuka, town hall, prisoners, and Oberst, he now had the further puzzlement of a French infirmary, and defeated British forces having left France. Admiral Carnaris? And who was Hitler that he deserved a Heil? And of course the face in the mirror!

He opened his eyes and again looked into the mirror. As he passed his hand over his forehead, the image looking back at him did the same in reverse, its fingers tracing over the scar, moving down the face to touch the mustache. Obviously the face in the mirror was his, yet it wasn't the face that he remembered. The scar could be the result of the shell blast, but obviously the fact that it was a well-healed scar and not a raw wound, and from the size of the scar possibly a serious wound, indicated that time had passed since its occurrence—considerable time. The other changes in the face also indicated the passage of time since his last remembrance. And from the look of the changes, again it had been a considerable passage of time.

He recalled that as a child, on a visit to his American grandparents living in Buffalo, in the state of New York, his maternal grandmother had read him the American folktale about someone who had awakened from a long sleep, one lasting several years. What was his name? Rip something, Rip Tide, no, Rip Twinkle, no, what did it matter what the name was. Ah yes, Rip Van Winkle. But that was a long sleep, a fairy tale. He had to have been awake during the passage of time since he had received the wound, perhaps for years. But he couldn't remember. *My God,* he thought. He couldn't remember! That thought triggered a remembrance. Somewhere in the back of his mind that seemed familiar. Sometime in the past he had had a similar problem.

Lessing told himself to calm down. He had to think rationally. Where could he start to resolve the puzzling questions? The French infirmary. He had a room all to himself. The doctor, the name Brachman, and his voice seemed familiar, and he had called him Wilhelm. Strange, for usually German doctors are rather formal, especially when addressing an Oberst, as this Wilhelm Lessing seemed to be. He had come running as soon as the major had called out. Well, the major had called him Oberst; probably one of this rank rated special attention. *But wait,* Lessing thought. On one of his excursions, disguised as German Lieutenant Lessing, he had contacted a Frenchman, an informant, who was working as an orderly at a German field hospital, a couple of miles behind the trenches. While the meeting took place outside the hospital building, Lessing had looked through the door into the hall, which was filled with wounded German soldiers lying on makeshift mattresses. If anything, the ferocity of the fighting had increased. Yet he had a room to himself.

Recollection continued in Lessing's mind. Oberst, the major and the doctor had called him—Oberst Lessing! A colonel! Could it be that the Germans had accepted his impersonation of Oberleutnant Lessing, accepting him into their army? The Lessing he could understand. He had had the name on the back of the captured Knights Cross blacked out and replaced with Wilhelm Lessing, a German variation of his real name. In case of trouble, he wouldn't have to remember a different name. But Oberst? Had he spent the passage of time, however long it was, in the German army, working his way up several ranks to colonel? Why would he do that? He mused. Was the war still in progress, several years later?

So many questions! Lessing thought. They might think he was Oberst Wilhelm Lessing, but he knew he was Lieutenant William Lessing of the British army. And he needed to get the answers to many questions. But carefully. As Oberst Lessing, he apparently was accepted and safe. If they found out he was Lieutenant Lessing, very likely he would be shot as a spy.

His thoughts were interrupted as the nurse reentered the room. Even in his present state of mind he couldn't help but notice her as a woman. She appeared to be about the same age as the face in the mirror, blond and very attractive for someone of her age, although perhaps a bit overweight for his taste. How did he know that?

She spoke with uncertainty in her voice, "Ah, you are awake again."

She paused for a long moment before continuing, "Oberst, I'll get the doctor."

Lessing replied in perfect unaccented German, "No, wait, please. What day is it?"

"Why, it's Friday. You were injured three days ago, last Tuesday."

"No, I mean what is the date?"

"June twenty-first."

"What year?"

"Oberst! Are you joking with me? Why, it's 1940, of course. Now I really must go and get Doctor Brachman."

As she left the room, Lessing closed his eyes again, stunned. June 1940! Almost twenty-two years! How was it possible that twenty-two years of his life had passed and he couldn't recall the passage of that time? The face in the mirror did look aged. What was that thought that he tried to recall, that he had had a few moments ago? A remembrance of another time when he couldn't remember.

Before he could weigh the fact that half of his life had passed without his knowledge, he heard someone enter the room. The man with the nurse was apparently the doctor. Doctor Brachman appeared to be a few years older than he was. And even more than the nurse, he had accumulated quite a few pounds over the years since he had last seen them. What was it that Lessing had just thought? Accumulated more pounds than the nurse? Had last seen them? He had seen them?

His thoughts were interrupted by the doctor. "How do you feel, Wilhelm? I imagine that once again you have quite a headache. The beam apparently hit you on the left side of your head in one of the same places where you were wounded back in 1918. It's quite a coincidence that we three meet again after so many years in much the same unfortunate—for you—circumstances. Fortunately, as was the case then, you apparently have only a concussion. Your skull appears to still be intact. Can you remember whether the pain is greater or lesser than it was then?"

With the acceleration of the accumulating facts about the confusing situation that Lessing found himself in, the pain had retreated to the back of his consciousness. However, Hans's question about it brought it back to the forefront of his attention. There was that fleeting remembrance again: where did Hans come from?

"It's pretty bad. But perhaps it is receding a bit. You spoke about the old wound in 1918. Frankly, Doctor, I'm having trouble remembering things."

The doctor took two tablets and a glass of water from the small tray that the nurse was carrying and handed them to Lessing. "Here, this should ease the pain. As I told you then, short-term loss of memory is not too uncommon with a head injury. Ideally, it won't be the complete autobiographical loss that you had before."

He bent over Lessing, shining a penlight into his eyes as he looked into them. "I see nothing alarming. However, this time if your memory loss lingers too long, we will have to send you to a specialist in Berlin. Treatment of autobiographical amnesia is now much more advanced than it was then. Let's see if you can stand up. And don't be so formal, Wilhelm. Twenty years ago, it was Hans, and so it should be now."

Amnesia! That helped to explain much. Hilga must be right. The doctor had said "twenty years ago." From 1918 to 1940 is twenty-two years! Lessing cautiously sat up, and then turned and gingerly placed his legs over the side of the bed. The nurse slid a pair of slippers onto his feet and helped him stand.

"I don't feel too weak," he said.

"Good. Our old friend Hilga will help you walk about a bit while I get someone to bring you something to eat. While you are eating, she will tell you about the victories we are achieving. Much different from our last meeting. This might help you regain your memory."

Lessing still knew nothing about the why and how of the present conflict. Surely it hadn't been going on for the twenty-plus years of his blacked-out memory! The last remembrance he had, way back in late October 1918, was that with the American army now in France and attacking in force, Germany was tottering on the brink of defeat. Now there were victories? As to where, apparently it was taking place in France. He decided it best to forgo asking questions, hoping that listening to the nurse would answer some of them.

As they returned to his room and he lay back down on the bed, she was gushing, having overcome the previous uncertainty in her voice. "The Führer himself will be accepting the defeat of the French at Compiegne today. Is it not glorious, Wilhelm, er, Oberst, that it is going to take place in the same railcar in which they humiliated the fatherland after the last war! With Poland, Holland, Belgium, Denmark, Norway, and now France at our fatherland's feet, we can now truly hold our heads high. And soon the haughty British will also kneel!"

Lessing closed his eyes and lay quietly. For the time being, having missed hearing the use of his given name, he assimilated what he had heard in his mind.

Hans had said he had amnesia from the 1918 wound, with complete loss of memory. Now, however, he could remember what had happened before the shell blast but was having trouble remembering what had happened in the intervening twenty-two years!

He thought, *It was indeed a different war, one that Germany appeared to be winning.* And in a very big way: Poland, Holland, Belgium, Denmark, Norway, and now France! The Allies had probably won the last one. But if they did, Lessing didn't remember it. Apparently he had become the victim of an acute and long-lasting case of amnesia. Not the short one that Hans thought he was probably now suffering. But the English were now losing! And what of the doctor? Hans seemed to know about his old wound and spoke as if they were old friends, dating back to 1918. He also seemed to know about his long-term amnesia. And he did remember a younger Hans from somewhere.

The nurse was continuing. "I hope you won't be offended that I know, Oberst, but the gossip from some of the wounded in the ward is that you and the major were interrogating the miserable English prisoners to secure information in preparation for our next victory: the invasion of England itself!"

More information. Apparently, as a German colonel, Lessing was involved in some kind of intelligence work, just as he had been more than twenty years ago—but good God, for the other side! Miserable English prisoners: that struck a chord. Bits and pieces were beginning to assimilate in his memory. He remembered an English prisoner. He, or rather Manz—he now remembered the major's name—had been interrogating an English prisoner just a few days ago. What was it that the prisoner had said? His middle initials, W, L, stood for William Lessing. The prisoner's middle names were the same as his!

For the next few minutes Lessing's mind shut out the voice of the nurse as it whirled with various scenarios of what might have happened those decades ago. There was, among others, one possible conclusion that could be reached: Penny was the only one who had died in the bus accident. Perhaps the unborn child had not also died when Penny had, but had survived. Perhaps he had a son, one whom he had never seen, hadn't even known he had. Jacob William Lessing Rosenstein's appearance and voice certainly had reminded him of someone—his younger self. Jacob William Lessing Rosenstein was quite possibly his son!

CHAPTER SIX

CHERBOURG, FRANCE
JUNE 21–22, 1940

Suddenly the pain in Lessing's head receded as he was overcome by a rush of remembrances. He knew he was William Lessing, a lieutenant in the British army. Behind German lines, masquerading as a German Oberleutenant, in 1918 seeking information for a dawn offensive. Apparently he was now also Wilhelm Lessing, twenty-two years later in 1940, Oberst in the Abwehr, the German counterintelligence service. He and Manz were interrogating French and English prisoners of war. As the nurse prated on about the glorious victories, Lessing closed his eyes, shutting out her droning voice, outwardly seeming to sleep.

The remembrances of his two lives—one as an Englishman and the other as a German—were tumbling out of his subconscious mind like the rushing waters of the Niagara River that he remembered from his childhood visit to New York State. Having first been split by Goat Island, the river roared over the American and Canadian falls as two separate crashing cataracts, one in one country and the other in the other, only to combine again into one river in the swirling waters below. It was as if the personal-memory portion of his brain had been split into two halves, each containing the remembrances of two different twenty-year-long time periods, and now a bridge was being constructed over the swirling waters in his mind, connecting the two.

The English remembrance and deductions were that just before he went over the line and was wounded, he had received the news that his wife, Penny, had died in an accident in her eighth month of pregnancy. He knew that his older sister, Martha, had married Jacob Rosenstein in 1915. Joining these were the recent German remembrances: three days earlier, Manz had interrogated a young English lieutenant, also with the name Rosenstein, first name Jacob, whose middle names were William Lessing and whose voice and looks reminded him of someone, who said his mother, Penny, had died in childbirth, who had then been adopted by his aunt Martha and his uncle Jacob Rosenstein, whose wife, Lessing was sure, was his sister Martha.

These were not astonishing coincidences. And with this good news, the remembrances of his English years were returning, combining with those of his German. *But is it good news?* he wondered. He had found that he probably had a son, which for years he hadn't even known he had. But this son was a prisoner of war. Taken prisoner by his army. Or was it his army? Which army was his? British or German? The whirlpool of returning, conflicting remembrances combined with the continuing throbbing pain in his head was too much, and lulled by the droning voice of the nurse, he again sank into a semi-unconscious state.

He was suddenly brought back to the present when Hilga stopped her narrative as Hans reentered the room. He was escorting an orderly with a tray of food. Lessing was suddenly ravenous. Hilga started to feed him, but he waved her aside, telling both of them that he was feeling fine and needed to get back on duty.

Hans replied, "Good, but I recommend that you stay here until tomorrow morning. If you are feeling well, we three can have breakfast together and bring one another up-to-date since we parted those many years ago." He left, as did Hilga after she had helped Lessing onto another bed by a window. A few minutes later, the door, which she had closed, opened, and Manz entered the room, saying, "The doctor says you will be able to leave tomorrow after breakfast. I'll leave now and go back to the town hall and finish my reports on our assignment. What time do you want me to pick you up?"

Lessing had been mulling over his dual life with his thoughts in his English mind. The sudden German words in Manz's somewhat harsh voice jerked him back to the present. He had trouble bringing his mind back to being the German Oberst. He was silent for more than a minute, causing Manz to say, with the same concern in his voice that had been there earlier, "Oberst, shall I call the doctor?"

Lessing, having altered his thoughts back into German replied, "I'm all right. Very good, Major. Make it use 09:30. And we will head back to headquarters." After Manz left, Lessing lay there as his mind continued to join his two lives together, now including his memories of a great deal of his early life. As darkness finally arrived on the longest daylight day of the year, the summer solstice, he once again drifted into a dream-filled sleep. Strangely, he remembered it in both the third and first person, as though his mind amid all the turmoil still couldn't completely accept who he really was.

CHAPTER SEVEN

WILLIAM LESSING'S LIFE,
1897–1918

Lessing's father, William Lessing, of the same name as his son, had been a high-level diplomat in the British Foreign Service. His mother was an American from New York State, whom his father had met when he had been posted to the American capital, Washington, during the last years of Queen Victoria's reign. William Lessing Jr. had actually been born in Washington, DC, in 1896. He was given the same name as his father, and following a long family tradition, the reason long forgotten, no middle name.

William Sr. had believed he could best do his job by getting to know the people of the countries to which he was posted as much as he could. This is how he had met his wife, Jennifer Seeley, the daughter of a congressman from western New York State.

His subsequent lengthy postings, first in Germany, then in France, with a shorter posting in Portugal in between, had subjected his son to these countries' cultures. Contrary to the practice of most British diplomats of the time, he had believed in immersing his two children, William Jr. and his sister, Martha, who was three years William's senior, into the culture of the visited country as much as possible. He did this by sending them to local schools and encouraging them to make friends with the "natives." William Jr.

apparently had an easygoing disposition and enjoyed making new friends. And they reciprocated. William Jr. had been quick to learn languages and during these years had learned to speak, read, and write German quite fluently and French and Portuguese to a lesser proficiency.

However, their national origin was not neglected. During summer vacations they spent time with their paternal grandparents in England and every other year in New York State with their maternal grandparents. When they were ready to enter college, they each were sent to England to further their education. William Jr. went to Cambridge University, and Martha went to a women's college, also in the city of Cambridge.

When the family left Germany when William Jr. was a teenager, the move to France was fortuitous, because in the next few years his physical appearance changed quite a bit. He had been a relatively small boy, with a rather round, chubby face. But in those few years in France he had grown appreciably in both height and breadth. His hair, which had been dark blond, darkened to a deep black, and his face lost its chubbiness and became somewhat elongated. So great was the change that anyone comparing pictures of the thirteen-year-old boy and the twenty-year-old young man would have had to look very closely to see that they were one and the same person.

Probably because of this change in his appearance, enhanced by the forehead scar and the mustache, no one in Lessing's later years in Germany after the war had recognized him as the son of a British diplomat. Such a recognition could have had dire repercussions for him.

Lessing's younger years in Germany had made a lasting impression on him. Therefore when he entered Cambridge at the age of eighteen, he majored in German literature and culture. Unfortunately, because England went to war with Germany shortly after he entered Cambridge, he had been unable to enhance his studies by spending time in Germany. Again, for his future well-being, that was probably fortuitous.

In 1916, at the age of twenty, having finished his second year at Cambridge, Lessing enlisted in the army. Because of his fluency in French and German and the university studies, he was used in analyzing and gathering intelligence information. It was in this role that he was sent over the German lines on that late October evening in 1918, which set the course for the rest of his life.

Lessing had met his future wife, Winifred Penelope (Penny) Bradford, while he was at Cambridge. His sister, Martha, in 1915 had married a former Cambridge student, Jacob Rosenstein. He was a young banker and the son of a Jewish businessman who was a longtime friend of the liberal Lessing family.

Penny was the daughter of one of his professors, James Bradford, who was a widower. Lessing and Penny married just before he entered the army. She was in the eighth month of her first pregnancy, having joined her husband's parents in their apartment in Paris. Hit by a bus, which precipitated the premature birth of their child, Penny was taken to a Paris hospital, but delivery complications caused by the accident had ensued, and she had died.

Lessing had been at the front assimilating information about the next morning's attack when the message telling of her death reached him. The brief message hadn't mentioned either the particulars of the accident or the premature birth of their son, just that she had died as the result of an accident. Because the child had not been due for several weeks, not knowing otherwise, he had assumed that it, too, had died.

Almost overcome by the appalling news, he had deliberately relegated it to the back of his mind, blocking it out as he continued his analysis of the information needed for the coming offensive. He had determined that they needed more information about the German defensive position and had convinced his commanding colonel that yet another intelligence-gathering excursion behind the enemy's lines was warranted. And that it was he, again assuming his role of Oberleutenant Wilhelm Lessing, who should make the excursion.

CHAPTER EIGHT

CHERBOURG, FRANCE
JUNE 22, 1940

It was getting light in the hospital room when Lessing awoke from his dream-filled sleep. The dreams he had had helped him make some sense out of the two fragmented portions of his life. With the only light coming from the setting moon, streaming through the windows, and a nightlight on one of the walls, the near darkness and the quietness of early day in the hospital acted as a balm to his seething mind. He was hungry and was tempted to call out to a nurse. Hilga? But caution prevailed. While he was alone, he thought, he had to try to make sense of his situation.

He rationalized why this revelation of his two lives had occurred at this time. As theorized by Hans years earlier, it had been the 1918 head wound that his subconscious mind had used as an excuse to relegate the horrible remembrance of a personal tragedy, the sudden deaths of his beloved Penny and their unborn child, into the deepest recesses of his mind. Twenty-two years later, the same subconscious part of his mind had put two and two together, and again using a hit to his head as the excuse, brought to the front of his mind the good news that their unborn child had survived the accident. With it had come the complete remembrance of his life before that day in 1918.

In his mind he enumerated what he now knew about William/ Wilhelm Lessing. Even though he had spent the last twenty-two years—most of his adult life—as a German, he suddenly realized that his thoughts were now in English. In the English language, his mind enumerated his situation:

1. For a long period he was a German, Wilhelm Lessing, with his life as William Lessing, the Englishman, hiding somewhere in the far recesses of his mind. Twenty-two years earlier, as he was recovering in a German hospital from a battle wound, he had been accepted as a wounded German officer because of the uniform and the Knights Cross he was wearing. The fact that he could speak perfect unaccented German reinforced the illusion.

   Because of the confusion of defeat, the fact that there wasn't a real Uberleutenant Wilhelm Lessing had gone undetected. His amnesia had also shielded him from this fact. He had thought he was indeed Wilhelm Lessing, born and raised in Germany. With his past life unremembered, he was a victim of prolonged autobiographical amnesia.

   For the past five years he had been an intelligence officer, and was now a colonel, in the Abwehr, the German counterintelligence service. Before that, he had been in the reconstituted army, the transfer coming two years after Hitler had come into power in 1933. He spent six years as an instructor at the school in Zurich. Not surprisingly, the recruitment officer in 1929 could find no army records for an Oberleutenant Wilhelm Lessing, since of course there had never been one. However, this wasn't considered too unusual, as the Allied powers mandated almost complete dissolution of the German army after the war, resulting in many records being lost. His only identifications had been the Knights Cross with "Wilhelm Lessing" on its back and the hospital records listing him as an Oberleutenant. The years between teacher and captain were spent as an arms salesman for the Fuerst Company.

Even though he was in his midthirties (he didn't know his exact age) and it had been fifteen years since his army experience, this had been enough for him to get a commission as an officer. Apparently his unremembered experience in the British army was another one of the learned skills that was unaffected by his amnesia. He felt the army was beginning to become the tool of the Nazis' SS. As a junior officer, there was nothing he could do about it. He knew he wouldn't be allowed to resign.

As Wilhelm Lessing during this period of his life, he had been a dedicated German officer with a German mind. Along with most Germans, he thought the Allied powers had treated Germany severely after the war. With no remembrances of happenings before October 1918, his knowledge of the cause of the war was based almost solely on his association with Germans and German postwar writings. And although he was rather well-off in his position at the school in Zurich, he had seen the results of the Weimar Republic's inability to pull Germany out of its postwar problems.

As a senior officer with Canaris, he had associated with people from other countries and been exposed to their views on the subject. He had generally taken these views with a grain of salt, considering them nothing more than the nationalistic views of the nationals making them. He had at first approved of the way Hitler had established himself as a strong leader. After the ineffectiveness of the Weimar Republic, he believed a firm hand at the head of state was a good thing. However, he was disturbed by the twists in the government's actions that had been occurring in the past few years.

2. He was also Lieutenant William Lessing—at least twenty-two years ago he had been, for two years a British army officer, wounded in battle in late 1918—although probably as far as the British army was concerned, he was missing in

action and presumed dead. He now remembered that he was the son of a high diplomat for the British government. Although he had spent most of his first twenty years in foreign countries, he had been raised as a British citizen with all the tradition and love of country and things British that that entailed. On his father's side of the family, he had been British, seemingly for centuries; on his mother's side, American and before that also British. His many early years of living in Germany had made it difficult for him to face Germans as enemies, but as an Englishman, it had been his duty as a soldier, and he had done it without the slightest hesitation. Fortunately, he had never encountered any German friends or even acquaintances during his time at the front.

3. His wife, Penny, had died in an accident, but apparently their child, a son, had survived. Presumably with his mother dead and his father missing in action and also presumed dead, the son had been adopted by Lessing's sister, Martha, and her husband, Jacob Rosenstein, a Jewish friend of the family. Of his son he knew nothing, except that he apparently had been given the name of his sister Martha's husband, had joined the British army, and was now a young British officer and a prisoner of the German army.

4. What could he do about his son's situation? It was bad enough that he was a prisoner of war, but his adopted name probably made his situation even worse. He was aware of Manz's notation of those prisoners who had Jewish-sounding names. And Rosenstein was certainly one of those. Although he was aware that Jacob William Lessing Rosenstein wasn't Jewish, and probably Manz was too, as he was there when the prisoner said his father's name was Lessing, those who might be reviewing and taking action from Manz's list wouldn't know that.

Or did Manz think that? Manz knew that the English lieutenant's aunt Martha had married a man with a Jewish name and therefore he probably was Jewish. Would Manz think that she had married a Jewish man because one or both of her parents were Jewish? If that were the case, Manz would think that the English lieutenant had Jewish blood flowing through his veins. And Jewish lineage passed through the mother. He hadn't noticed whether Manz had had the notation put after Jacob W. L. Rosenstein's name. The Kristalnacht syndrome and other unnecessary repressive actions of Hitler's rule were the governmental twists he didn't like. Like most of Canaris's staff, he was aware of the conflict between Canaris's Abwehr and Himmler's Gestapo. This conflict was probably the reason why Himmler had insisted that Manz, one of Himmler's men, work with Lessing in the interrogation of the prisoners.

As Oberst Lessing, he, like most of his fellow officers, believed the English, French, and Poles they were fighting, although the enemy, were still men, and until proven otherwise, were to be considered honorable men. When they were captured, they should be treated as Germans would want German soldiers to be treated if they were captured. However, many of Himmler's minions, and this quite possibly included Manz, believed that such a policy didn't necessarily apply to certain "non-Aryan" prisoners. And such beliefs were not restricted to captured enemy soldiers; also included were unarmed civilians and even, oftentimes, Germans.

Although as far as he knew, Jewish war prisoners were not yet being singled out for "ethnic cleansing," this didn't mean that they wouldn't be in the future. Consequently, he had especially strong motives for doing something about his son's situation.

5. But why should he? He now was almost positive that Jacob was his son, but he didn't know him as an individual. A

few days ago, he hadn't even known he had a son, much less a British one. A few minutes' contact in an adversarial situation, during which he had shown strong character, still hardly told him what his son was really like. He had apparently been raised by his sister, Martha. However, he certainly knew her; at least he had twenty-two years earlier. And if Jacob was anything like Martha, that was all to the good.

And there were his parents. Father had still been representing the British government, living with Mother in Paris. And during the final months of her pregnancy, Penny had been staying with them when he made that fateful excursion over the lines in 1918. Surely they must have also been involved in the formative years of their grandson's life. If they were still alive. Were they? They would be in their late sixties now. And what of James Bradford, Penny's father and William's other grandfather? Also surely he would have been involved with his grandson's upbringing. So many questions to be answered!

6. Hilga! The nurse was Hilga Regensburg! His nurse in the hospital all those years ago. His two minds for a moment relished the memory of that night so long ago. But only for a moment, for that night was only a few weeks after Penny's tragic death. Mentally he rebuked his stupid subconscious mind for allowing such misbehavior. But was it stupid? For one night, at least, something pleasant was occurring in his bewildered amnesia life.

For God's sake, Lessing, let it go. It happened two decades ago.

Fortune was on his side, for at that moment the room's door opened and a nurse entered with a tray, on which was a pot of coffee. She opened the room's closet, and, pointing to his uniform that was hanging in it, said, "The doctor will be in soon. If he approves, you can get dressed."

44

CHAPTER NINE

GERMANY

DECEMBER 1918–JUNE 1919

Lessing didn't spend all his evenings discussing his amnesia problem with Doctor Hans Brachman. By December 1918 when he was working as an orderly at the hospital near Bonn, he had recovered from his physical wounds if not his mental ones. Even though he didn't remember his past, he was fully aware of the needs and desires of a young man in his twenties.

Hilga Regensburg was also in her twenties and attractive. She had married a young man three years older than her own age, twenty, in the spring of 1914. He had almost immediately been called into the army. When her husband entered the army, she decided to also serve her country by becoming a nurse. By 1918, she had become a skilled practitioner of her profession, achieving the rank of matron, or head nurse. She had been at the field hospital near the front for more than a year. The hospital's proximity to the fighting enabled her to occasionally see her husband, who had by late 1918 become an Unteroffizier. Only hours before the shell landed, the two of them had had a hasty romantic interlude together in her quarters. Unfortunately for her, he had been the Unteroffizier that Lieutenant Lessing had observed just before the shell landed. She already knew this when she first met Lessing in the ward.

The shell that had given him his amnesia had also made her a war widow. That may have been why she seemed to be in a disturbed state of mind at that first meeting. Lessing, having been wounded by the same shell that had made her a widow strangely seemed to draw her nearer to him. Perhaps as a substitute for Konrad. The task of caring for the large patient contingent left little time for outside activities. All the hospital's undermanned staff, including doctors, nurses, and orderlies, were working seven days a week and twelve-plus hours a day. During what breaks there were, Hilga occasionally sought out the bewildered Lessing, finding comfort in her loss by consoling him in his. Those evenings when she wasn't on duty she spent alone in the small single room provided for her as head nurse. When the bandages were removed from her lieutenant patient, her nursing experience allowed her to overlook the large healing scar on his forehead and see that he was indeed a handsome, well-built young man. Surprisingly, she thought, in appearance he was a lot like her Konrad.

By then she knew that the shell that had killed her husband had also probably been the one that had given Lessing his wounds. She would have been justified in feeling resentment that Lessing had lived while Konrad had been killed, but to the contrary, she felt an attraction toward him. Her years of seeing the carnage and butchery that the trench warfare produced seemed to deaden the reality of her loss.

Perhaps because he seemingly had no past and, at least in her mind, seemed to have a physical resemblance to her Konrad, she began to see in him, if not a replacement, at least a substitute for her fallen soldier. Her nurse friends apparently felt that she wished to be alone in the grief of her loss.

Her room was next door to the quarters of Hans Brachman. She heard Lessing as he passed by and entered Brachman's quarters. The thin walls of the building enabled her to hear their muffled voices as they discussed Lessing's problems.

One evening she heard him knocking on Brachman's door and there was no answer. Knowing that Brachman would be away for the night, she had, unbeknownst to Lessing, made arrangements for a clandestine meeting. As he turned away from Brachman's door, she, clad only in a loosely tied cotton robe, opened hers and invited him in for a drink from a freshly opened bottle of Ahrweiler red wine.

When Lessing left in the early morning, she was still asleep. When she woke up a few hours later, she was shocked at her actions so soon after Konrad's death. She changed her attitude toward Lessing, and their relationship became that of a head nurse and a lowly orderly. With the war over and lost, his former rank of lieutenant was forgotten. Lessing also sensed that in spite of his sexual needs, what had happened was unseemly. He accepted her change in attitude without comment to her. They never repeated the performance during the remaining few weeks of his stay at the hospital. Later that month Hilga missed her period. At first she didn't think about it too much, thinking that it was probably because of the shock of Konrad's death and the end of the war. She deliberately ignored her night with Lessing. By the second month, however, the changes in her body were apparent to her, and she knew she was pregnant. She and Konrad had specifically tried not to have a child. Accordingly they had taken the precautions against pregnancy that were available at the time. They thought the uncertainty of war and the need to put the welfare of their country first, to have her available full time as a nurse, precluded starting a family until the war was over. She had not taken the same precautions during her passionate night with Wilhelm Lessing.

She was sure that the child was his. By that time, however, he was gone to some place—she knew not where. By the fourth month, her condition was evident to all. Her fellow workers, not aware of the precautions that she and Konrad had taken, assumed the child was the result of their last night together before his deadly rendezvous with the fateful shell. They were unaware of the clandestine meeting and did not know the expected date of birth. Hilga, however, of course knew the arithmetic of pregnancy, and in June 1919, her sixth month, she left the hospital and returned to the home of her parents on a farm in the small village of Aitern in the Black Forest in the hills south of the city of Freiburg and near

Germany's borders with Switzerland and France. Her mother and father, Wilhelmnina and Max, also assumed the child was Konrad's. It was a girl, who was given the name of her mother, Hilga, with of course the surname of her supposed father, Regensburg, and the middle name of Wilhelmnina, after Hilga's mother. They were quite proud of the professional achievement of their nurse daughter and accepted without question her contrived medical explanation of the reason for the unexpectedly lengthy pregnancy.

CHAPTER TEN

SCHWARZWALD (BLACK FOREST)
GERMANY
SEPTEMBER 1929, 1940

For ten years, Hilga had raised Wilhelmnina as a single mother. Continuing to live with her parents and her brother Leopold, who was five years younger, on the farm, she had been able to secure the position of head nurse at the hospital in the small town of Schonau, a two-mile walk from Aitern. The family's home was constructed like most of the area's farmers': a house with the barn for the farm's animals on the ground floor and the family's living quarters on the second. In the cold winters, the warmth generated by the animals helped heat the living quarters above. Living rent-free on the farm, which supplied more than enough food for the family now numbering five, she and her young daughter were able to survive quite well in those troubled times, including the out-of-control inflation that was Germany's fate during the aftermath of the war. With a sense of guilt over the circumstances surrounding her child's birth, she had abstained from all but the most casual social association with men.

Hans Brachman, who was a few years older than Hilga, had first met her at the field hospital in 1917. He was initially attracted to her because of her physical beauty. However, working with her professionally, he soon learned that there was much more to Hilga Regensburg than the pleasant contours of her body, the shape of her face, and the sheen of her blond hair, which were the envy of the other nurses. Respecting her marriage to a soldier fighting at the front, he had abstained from any unseemly acts, treating her only as a fellow medical professional and a friend. Within six months after Hilga left the hospital near Bonn, its few remaining patients had been sent either home or to hospitals nearer their homes.

Brachman had returned to Munich, where he was reunited with Maria, a young woman he had known before the war. However, the relationship lasted less than a year. Brachman was troubled by the violence that was happening in the city. He attended the February Beer Hall Putsustary in 1920 and was deeply disturbed by Hitler's comments, which lasted for more than two hours. Maria did not attend the meeting, but her father did, and she was impressed by his praise for what Hitler said and his report of the enthusiasm the two thousand attendees had shown for Hitler's presentation. The 1923 killings were too much for Hans. So in January 1924, upon hearing a surgeon was needed in a village hospital in the Schwarzwald, he resigned at the hospital where he was chief surgeon, bid good-bye to Maria, and moved to Schonau.

CHAPTER ELEVEN

CHERBOURG, FRANCE
JUNE 22, 1940

The doctor, nurse, and patient sitting at a table in the hospital's dining room were silent as the commandeered French waiter cleared away the breakfast dishes, leaving cups of coffee for his conquerors. Hans had been cheerful from the moment they had sat down. Lessing's attitude was somewhat reserved, but not primarily for the reason that his tablemates assumed, which was his near clash with possible death, but because of the problem of his double identity. As the meal progressed, Hans gave a condensed version of his trials and tribulations of the preceding twenty-two years, including the past fourteen, which he and Hilga had spent together as doctor and nurse at the hospital in Schonau and as good friends outside those hours, she living with her parents and he in the suite that the hospital supplied for its chief surgeon. He didn't include any specifics. Even though he and Lessing had been close, the relationship had been limited because of terrible months of defeat two decades earlier. Oddly, they had not met during the twenty-two years that followed.

Lessing had too much on his mind to be very interested in the lives of two Germans. However, he knew he had to seem interested, to camouflage his identity problem. And, after all, these two people had served him well, and they did seem to be nice.

When Hilga began, Lessing noticed that she seemed apprehensive, probably for two reasons. For one, she was having an informal meal with an Oberst in the German spy army. Secondly, of course, was the night she and Lessing had shared so many years ago, which now joined the horde of memories that Lessing was recalling.

Hilga related that she and Konrad, to her lifelong joy, had one night a few days before his death romanced, at which time they had conceived their daughter. Noticing her somewhat anxious manner as she spoke rapidly and avoided looking at him, Lessing recalled her similar attitude when they had first met a few days earlier. Hearing her parenting tale, Lessing was dealt another shock: the realization that he, not Konrad, probably had a daughter!

Fortunately Hans was looking at her, so neither one of them noticed that Lessing's body suddenly tensed as he realized that he had fathered not just one but two children.

When she finished her history, a few sentences later, Hans turned to Lessing, anticipating the beginning of his recitation about the past two decades of his life. Seeing his tensed body, he asked, with alarm in his voice, "What's the matter, Wilhelm? You suddenly look worse."

Inwardly gritting his teeth, Lessing successfully made his body relax, enabling him to reply. At that moment, the hospital's dining hall clock chimed the half hour and the ever-efficient Manz appeared in the doorway. "Nothing—just that it's late and Manz is waiting."

A few minutes were enough for him to relate his experience as a teacher at the school. This was followed by a short history of the salesman years for Fuerst's firm, followed by his return to the military. He left out unpleasant happenings while overemphasizing the good ones. Struggling with the turmoil in his mind, including his feelings about the information he had learned a few minutes earlier, he tried to act like an officer in a triumphant army.

Rising, Lessing thanked Hans and Hilga for their help, but said he had to go. He followed Manz out of the building, where a uniformed soldier was holding the rear door of an army vehicle open. Manz stepped aside, and as Lessing got into the rear seat, followed by Manz, he mulled over in his mind that this was his first experience in the dual role as a German officer and a British soldier. *Was he a British soldier?* he wondered. After all, he had been in the German army since 1929, more than eleven years.

Lessing listened as Manz explained how he had spent most of the two days that his Oberst had been unconscious, compiling and coordinating the results of the hundreds of interrogations they had conducted. He pointed to the front seat, which was filled with file boxes. From one of them he extracted a well-filled folder and handed it to Lessing.

"Well done, Major," Lessing said as he leafed through what he guessed was more than fifty pages. "This will keep me busy on the flight back to Hamburg. When will we get there?"

"We'll get to the plane in a few minutes," Manz replied. "It is waiting for us."

A sudden remembrance gripped Lessing: Jacob! The cause of his present situation. He hadn't given him a thought since his discovery of who he really was.

"By the way, Major, where was that last batch of prisoners sent—the one who had W. L. as his middle initials?" he said with a slight grin.

"They are being transported to a prisoner-of-war camp in Belgium, using the usual form of transport by train. Depending on both the distance to travel and the number of times the train will have to be shunted onto a siding to make way for a passing troop train, they should be there within a week."

They completed the journey to the plane in silence. Lessing appeared to be absorbed in the folder's contents. However, his mind was 100 percent occupied with contemplating what his next step should be. With a minimum of conversation on the plane, his mulling continued. By the time the plane touched down in the late afternoon, he had made up his mind.

They were greeted by a sergeant, who drove them to their quarters. Lessing's was a two-room suite and Manz's just one room.

On the way, the driver said that the admiral would see them at 09:00 the next morning and that this would give the Oberst the opportunity to get a good rest after his ordeal of the past two days. As the two of them were served their dinner, Lessing continued leafing through the folder, discussing its contents with Manz. As they left the dining hall, Lessing commeted, "Very good, Major, but it still needs to be condensed some more. Cut it down to not more than five or so pages. Do you have the use of a typewriter?" When Manz nodded, he continued, I'll see you at 06:00 for a final review before we see the admiral." Later in his quarters he continued his study well into the early morning before lying down for a few hours' sleep.

During the hours in his quarters, Lessing also weighed the options for his two different problems.

First was the immediate situation. For the time being at least, he had to continue to be (*Make that act as,* he thought) a German Oberst. He would prepare a report based on conclusions that the British forces and their allies had suffered a crushing defeat, and that even though the survivors were possibly still good soldiers, their vastly reduced numbers and the loss of their equipment and weapons meant that they were essentially nothing more than a weak home guard. They were no match for the well-trained, battle-experienced, and well-equipped German forces.

However, as a British officer he had to use caution in preparing the report. He had to reduce the magnitude of the British defeat in such a way that would give pause to Hitler's invasion plans. There was another problem; he had to be very careful in playing down the British defeat, for Manz was no fool. He would be looking over his shoulder.

Second, of course, was the other problem. What would Lessing do in the future? As he lay down to sleep, he weighed the pros and cons of what he would do. Waking up shortly before his meeting with Manz, Lessing quickly made up his mind. He would continue to be a German officer, but he would also be a British spy! He knew it would be difficult to achieve. And additionally there was the third problem: what about his son?

CHAPTER TWELVE

HAMBURG, GERMANY
JUNE 22, 1940

After spending almost two hours the next morning making a final review of Manz's efforts, the two of them arrived at the admiral's outer office promptly at nine o'clock. They were ushered by a uniformed sailor into Canaris's rather barren office. Other than his massive desk and chair, there were only six chairs around a large table, and a large filing cabinet alongside a large window that overlooked the harbor. However, there was a surprising sight. In one corner were two small dogs, lying in their box. Behind his desk, on the wall, was a large picture of Canaris speaking to Hitler. The German navy and Nazi flags flanked the picture. The latter was a deep red, with a white circle in the middle serving as the background for a black swastika.

Occupying three of the chairs were the admiral's second in command, Generalmajor Oster, Major Stenis, and Major Kompter. The former was a fellow member of the Admiral's inner circle, and the major was from Himmler's staff.

The admiral ordered the sailor to provide coffee. While the six of them spent several minutes drinking it with the usual greetings and military small talk, Lessing limited his part of the conversation to listening with both ears as these senior officers prated about military affairs that a British spy would die for, while sailors in the outer office were typing copies of Manz's report. The always efficient Manz had used carbon paper to make the needed six copies and had all his other papers in a small suitcase. *How did he know to make six?* Lessing thought.

The six gathered around the table, and without stopping for lunch, spent the next several hours going over the five-page report. Manz had concluded that the enemy's defeat, which included thousands of casualties and the loss of almost all their equipment and weapons, also lessened their ability to repel Germany's battle-hardened soldiers and superior equipment. Included within the report (by Lessing's suggestion to Manz) was a brief detail about the escape from Cherbourg Harbor of British soldiers loaded with military equipment. Lessing, while generally agreeing, downplayed the complete incapacity of the British, careful of how he did so. After all, he hadn't been part of the British armed forces for two decades.

Several hours later, the admiral, generally agreeing with Lessing's viewpoint, rose, saying, "Thank you all. I will take our recommendations to our leader tomorrow." He was being generous in his use of words, for the recommendations would exclude the others and be his alone.

As Manz, Hoffman, and Stenis rose, he continued to Lessing, "Oberst, please remain. The general and I want to talk to you."

When the other three had left, he motioned Lessing into one of the two other chairs that Oster pulled out from the table and placed by Canaris's desk. When seated, the admiral folded his hands on the desk and stared at Lessing for more than a minute, alarming him. Had Canaris figured out his dual identity? Surely not; it was impossible. He did not know himself a week ago. During the previous hours, Lessing had mentally marveled at his situation: a mere British lieutenant sitting at a table with high-ranking German officers discussing their military stratagem.

Finally, Wilhelm Canaris spoke. "Oberst, I have a special mission for you. To go over to the other side. I have observed your perfect English and other languages as you met with men on the other side before the war. I'm sure during those meetings you spoke their mother languages as if they were your own. I'm also sure you picked up enough mannerisms during those meetings to pass as an Englishman."

He paused, not speaking for a couple of minutes. During the silence, Lessing's mind was racing. He could hardly believe what he had just heard. It appeared that his decision to continue posing as a German officer while actually being in the English intelligence system was falling right into his lap.

Canaris finally spoke. "I want you to take a personal message, directly, to the English prime minister, Winston Churchill." He paused for a few seconds, and then said with a slight smile, "From Wilhelm to Winston and back to Wilhelm."

CHAPTER THIRTEEN

CANARIS'S OFFICE
JUNE 24, 1940, 6 PM

The admiral had assigned the development of the project to Majorgeneral Oster. After a quick meal, Lessing joined him in his office. As he entered, he was astonished to see Julian Fuerst bending over the table busily writing something. When the war started in 1939, the thirty-three-year-old heeded the call of his country and also, like Lessing several years earlier, left his father's company. It so happened that during the First World War, the senior Fuerst had met Reichmarine Captain Canaris, now Admiral Canaris. Not wanting his son to get into actual combat, he had asked Canaris to take Julian into his fold, which he did. It had quickly become apparent that Julian had abilities in planning various Abwehr activities.

What was the project? Canaris explained to Lessing that he and certain other ranking military officers wanted to end the war, to stop the killing. Canaris knew that Hitler did also. But, the admiral explained, not for the same reason.

With the fighting with England stopped, Hitler's plan was that Germany could then rid the world of communism by concentrating on attacking Russia. However, their information indicated that the conditions in Hitler's demands included having Germany retain control of all conquered areas and the return to Germany of all the former German territories outside Europe that were taken after the last war.

Canaris knew that Churchill would never agree to this. His group was willing to agree to limit territory acquisitions to those already taken. If that too was unacceptable to Churchill, as a last resort Canaris would have German troops leave Norway, Belgium, the Netherlands, and France, excepting the Ruhr. And because they had no love for Himmler and his SS, they were willing to throw him and even Hitler in as a bonus. Obviously the operation had to be done under a cloak of secrecy. If Hitler found out, it would be the end of Canaris.

First, Lessing the German, not as an Englishman, as Canaris had first considered, but as a Spaniard, would become a representative of Spain's dictator Franco, with his approval, speaking for certain German generals who along with Canaris wanted a truce with Britain. Lessing was to deliver a message asking for a meeting between them and Churchill.

The reason for this subterfuge was that it would allow Lessing to openly get into Britain as a neutral Spaniard. If this meeting didn't work out, Lessing could indeed become a spy for Germany, getting as much information about the status of the British armed forces as he could. However, this would be difficult. Although Franco would probably be willing to assist in arranging a truce, he was likely to object to using a member of his ambassadorial staff, which Lessing would be pretending to be, to remain in England as a spy. If the British found out, they quite likely would send the entire delegation back to Spain.

The foregoing was Canaris's plan, but it certainly was not Lessing's. He did intend to carry out the first step, even though it wouldn't be a German but an Englishman, speaking for Canaris through an imitation Spaniard diplomat. Lessing, however, would not remain as a spy for Germany if he failed to get the British to meet with Canaris and possibly end the war.

As the son and heir apparent of Heinrich Fuerst the Swiss industrialist, Julian would escort Lessing from Germany across the Swiss border to Zurich and then to Madrid. There, using Canaris's contacts with Franco and a considerable payment, in dollars not marks, to the dictator's representatives, he would arrange for not Wilhelm Lessing, a German, but José Solvanal, a Spaniard (Julian's recommendation), to be temporarily included in the staff of Spain's ambassador to the embassy in London.

Lessing was amazed at his young companion's skill in making the arrangements—much better than he could have done. Lessing had had contact with nationals from other countries, but that had been before 1939 and the start of hostilities. Also, although he actually was somewhat familiar with dealing with foreign delegations, that experience had been more than two decades ago when his father was a diplomat during a time of peace.

During their years together at the school in Switzerland, Lessing and Julian had become rather close. Julian had overcome his earlier problems and become a very good student. Because his mother was a German, he was able to join the army in 1933 at the same time Lessing had, entering as a private, of course. After joining Canaris, Oster had recommended to him that Julian Fuerst could become a valuable member of Canaris's Abwehr organization. Canaris had made Julian a member. Who quickly was indeed a big plus to the admiral's inner circle.

There was considerable discussion about the kind of message Lessing would present to the British. And would it be a handwritten message or a a typed one? It was finally decided that there would be two handwritten messages. The admiral wanted the messages to be perfect. He gave Lessing their content in German, which Lessing had translated into proper English. And in case they had to be destroyed, he, as Solvanal, could verbally recite them. The admiral then copied Lessing's translation in his longhand.

The first one identified the carrier of the messages as a Spaniard, José Solvanal, whom he had selected himself. The second read as follows:

To Prime Minister Churchill, I, Admiral Wilhelm Canaris, present the proposition that I meet with you to discuss the possibility of a truce between our two countries. I propose that there be no conditions before our meeting. Francisco Franco has agreed to our meeting in Spain, with you coming by way of Gibraltar. It is essential that our meeting be secret. No one here in Germany but Majorgeneral Oster, Oberst Lessing, my administrative assistant Julian Fuerst, and I know of this proposal. Francisco Franco knows of the meeting proposal and may guess its subject but cannot know for sure its purpose. Solvanal is authorized to bring your handwritten answer to me along with any suggestions or comments. He has been ordered to destroy the written messages if they are in danger of being taken from him.

Oster had given Lessing a sealed envelope, saying, "This envelope is waterproof. The messages are to remain there until you can hand it to Churchill. The admiral's messages have been written with a special ink on special chemically treated cloth that will appear to be blank and will begin to disintegrate if exposed to air. You must advise the prime minister that the envelope must—I repeat, must—be opened under water. The water will bring out the written messages quickly, within a minute, and will stiffen the cloth so air will not harm it. Perhaps you should say five minutes to be on the safe side. If for some reason you have to destroy the messages, rip open the envelope and throw the cloths into the air. They will appear to be blank and will quickly disintegrate. That action should be taken only as a last resort if someone other than Churchill gets them. And if you do destroy them, you know their contents, which you can verbally repeat to Churchill."

While he was speaking, Julian entered the room with a container of water and two envelopes. He set the container on a table and tossed one of the envelopes into it. When Oster finished speaking, Julian tore the other one open and handed two pieces of half-letter-sized sheets of cloth to Lessing. He was able to see only that they were blank before they began to crumble into dust.

Oster and Lessing looked on as he reached into the container and, holding the other envelope under water, tore it open, removed a piece of cloth, and spread it out on the bottom of the pail. Within a minute writing began to appear: "Oberst Wilhelm Lessing is off to London."

61

CHAPTER FOURTEEN

EN ROUTE
JUNE 27–JULY 1, 1940

The plan had been completed and was ready for implementation in two days. However, Canaris delayed its implementation for a day while he waited to see if Hitler was having any success in contacting the British. What his sources found out was that Herman Goring, the head of Germany's air force, was urging Hitler to start bombing London. Lessing spent the day updating his knowledge of Germany's war capability. In doing so, he explained it to Canaris and Oster so that he could convince Churchill, if necessary, of the futility of continuing the conflict. Of course the information would please Churchill!

On June 27, Julian and Lessing started to implement Lessing's journey to London, traveling by airplane to Madrid. Receiving the directive from Majorgeneral Oster, Major Pasht, who had replaced Lessing as the Abwehr's officer at the German embassy in Madrid, had made arrangements with Spanish officials, after a five-minute meeting with Franco, for Lessing's acceptance by Spain's ambassador to Britain, Gomez. They could have used perfect Spanish identification documents that the Abwehr technicians had prepared, but Julian was determined to have them use real documents. As Canaris's representative, he, with Peckeroth's help and the payment of a large amount of American dollars, not German marks, received authentic documents for José Solvanal prepared by Spanish technicians from the Spanish officials he was dealing with. He also made arrangements for the latter part of Lessing's trip.

With the envelope belted around his waist, the appropriate documents in a briefcase, and wearing clothes and having in a suitcase other personal items (no weapons) all bearing Spanish labels, Lessing as Oberst Lessing, acting as Solvanal, and Julian continued to implement Canaris's plan and one of Lessing's own. The first leg was taking the train to Lisbon. From there they journeyed to Dublin on a civilian airplane. Their route was south of the Channel Islands, which were, on that date, occupied by German forces.

As Julian was returning to Germany, he had arranged during their time in Madrid for one of the members of Spain's British ambassadorial delegation, who had been sent by Ambassador Gomez, to escort José Solvanal to London. He accompanied Lessing by ferry to Glasgow, Scotland. There British immigration officials reviewed their documents and, after intense analysis of Lessing's documents, allowed them to leave by train to London. They were met by an embassy employee with an automobile who drove them to the embassy in a century-old building.

Lessing was very curious about what London would look like, as it had been more than twenty years since he had been there. Observing the countryside on the train trip to London, he thought it didn't seem to have changed much. However, the developed part of the city seemed to be somewhat more changed from his remembrance. Approaching the city's center, he saw that there was a definite change in its appearance. Many of the buildings had sandbags piled around their entrances. The driver of the automobile advised Lessing, in Spanish, that the city was blacked out from sunset to sunrise. Military personnel were everywhere. Lessing noticed that there were very few children, even though it was a weekend. The driver told him that children had been evacuated from most parts of the city to the countryside, because it was anticipated that the Germans would soon start bombing the city. Food already was being rationed, but the embassy did not have a problem since the staff could import food by air from Portugal. Although there had not been any bombing of the city yet, Lessing knew that Hitler would probably, at Goring's encouragement, soon begin his barrage. He mused that perhaps the report that he had prepared for Canaris would to some degree encourage Hitler to start the bombing, because downplaying the actual seriousness of the evacuations from the French Coast meant that the British might need to be more demoralized.

José Solvanal was greeted by Ambassador Roberto Gomez, who escorted the German Oberst, acting as a Spaniard, José Solvanal (only Lessing acting as the German Oberst Lessing, knew that he was actually an Englishman) to his elaborate office, furnished with tables, chairs, and desks. With the two of them enclosed by themselves in the office, Lessing as Oberst Lessing revealed, in Spanish, the purpose of his coming to London: the arrangement of a possible meeting between the German generals and Admiral Canaris with appropriate British officials for the development of a peace treaty.

Lessing kept to himself the two other potential reasons for his journey to Britain. First was the Abwehr fallback. If the proposal meeting could not be arranged, Oberst Lessing, using his Spanish identity, would spy for Canaris, getting as much military information as he could before he returned to Germany with Churchill's refusal—which of course Lessing wouldn't do. And second would be revealing his true identity to the British officials. Gomez had been advised by Franco that a German posing as a Spaniard would temporarily be a member of his staff. However, he was not told why. Upon learning the purpose of the visit, he was angry that he had not been selected by Canaris and Franco as the one to meet with the appropriate British officials, whom he already knew and with whom he had had discussions about problems and arrangements between the two countries.

Lessing calmed him down by saying that he, the Canaris representative, knew many of the German personnel involved and that his perfect understanding and use of the English language would enable him to decipher any hidden meaning the British might have. As Oberst Lessing, he waved aside Gomez's question about how he had acquired this perfect tool for negotiating with the British, not explaining that he had acquired this phenomenon as the son of a British diplomat, speaking perfect English and Spanish and the ability to ferret out military secrets. Gomez took Lessing to a small suite—an office and sleeping facilities—telling him that he would arrange a confidential meeting with the appropriate British officials, ideally including Churchill. He advised Lessing to stay in the building until he had made the appropriate arrangements.

CHAPTER FIFTEEN

LONDON, ENGLAND
JULY 2, 1940

Lessing, as José Solvanal, was standing in the cramped reception area of Great Britain's foreign office, part of the underground headquarters of Winston Churchill. He was waiting to be escorted into the office of (although he didn't know it) seventy-one-year-old William Lessing, who, having been called out of retirement when the war started, was using his years of experience in prewar Germany to advise Winston Churchill.

The older Lessing was surprised that someone from the Spanish ambassadorial delegation wanted to talk to him. Years earlier, he had had contact with Spaniards, but the name José Solvanal didn't strike a chord in his memory. He rose from behind his desk as the foreign diplomat entered the room. Dropping back into his chair with a look of bewilderment, he stared at his visitor's face. The man seemed familiar, but his hair was longer, and his face had a mustache and age lines on it. *No, it can't be ... ,* he thought.

Lessing was as surprised as he was by the coincidence that the British official Gomez had arranged for him to see was William Lessing the elder, whom he hadn't seen for more than two decades. (Gomez, of course, knew him only as a German.) Quickly recovering, the younger Lessing greeted Lessing Sr. "Hello, Father," he said. He nodded toward the secretary to close the office door and strode over behind the desk, bent over, and lifted the shocked, somewhat smaller father into his arms. After holding him for a minute or so, he gently lowered him back into the chair and said, "Please tell your secretary that you don't want any interruptions for the next hour."

The younger Lessing pulled up and sat down in a chair next to his father's. He poured him a glass of water from a pitcher on a nearby table, saying as he did so, "Yes, even though I'm sure you will find it hard to believe, it is me. Just sit there and I will relate the unbelievable."

For the next hour or so, the younger related to the elder the fantastic events of the past two decades of his life, ending with the really beyond-belief reason he was in Britain. He was not there as a German spy or returning to Britain as a British soldier; he was there as a representative of Admiral Canaris and certain German generals, hoping to arrange an armistice between their two countries—the objective he had decided took priority over all the others.

When Lessing finished, there was a lengthy period of silence. When his father seemed about to speak, he quickly continued, "And we have a big personal problem, involving both good and bad news. Your grandson is alive; however, he is a prisoner of war."

For a long period of time as Lessing watched him, his father was again silent. After what seemed an eternity, he picked up his telephone and said into it, "Place a security guard outside the office." Then he turned to his son and said, "What you just told me is the most ridiculous thing I have ever heard. You want me to believe that you are the son I lost twenty years ago. True, you do perhaps have a resemblance to how he might look at this time. But even if you are my long-lost son, your tale indicates that for more than twenty years—half of your life, almost all of your adult life—you believed you were a German officer. How do I know you're not representing a German with some plot against Britain?"

Lessing was shocked at his reaction, but realizing it was quite a tale, he replied, "Father, please calm down. I can understand your not believing it. To reinforce my case, if you will bear with me, I'll relate my remembrances of my early life. I was named after you, Father, and as was the case with you, I was given no middle name—a family tradition going back several generations. And as I was growing up, you were a high-level diplomat in the British Foreign Service. You married Mother, an American." Pausing from his tale, he asked, "How is Mother?"

"She's all right. She was devastated when Penny was killed. Then when we heard you were Missing-in- action, we were both devastated. The birth of Jacob eased the pain a bit, but we have grieved ever since. Now, continue."

"She's from New York State. You met her when you were posted to the American capital, Washington, during the last years of Queen Victoria's reign. I was born in Washington, in 1896. You believed you could best do your job by getting to know the people of the countries to which you were posted as much as you could. This is how you met Mother, Jennifer Seeley, the daughter of a congressman from western New York State. Your subsequent lengthy postings, first in Germany and then in Spain and France, and in between a shorter posting in Portugal, subjected me to these countries' cultures. Contrary to the practice of most British diplomats of the time, you also believed in immersing your children—my sister, Martha, and me—into the local culture. Which you did."

A loud knocking on the door interrupted Lessing. His father held up his hand, rose from his chair, walked to the door, and opened it. The middle-aged woman who was his secretary whispered into his ear and escorted him through the door, closing it behind her. Lessing picked up a glass and poured himself a drink of water. Time passed, and the door remained shut. Beginning to become alarmed by the lengthy absence, the younger Lessing was reaching for the pitcher to pour another drink of water when the door opened and his father came in, followed by another elderly man whom Lessing almost instantly …

CHAPTER SIXTEEN

LONDON, ENGLAND
JULY 1, 1940

James Bradford was depressed. A widower whose only daughter, Penelope, had died in an accident in Paris more than two decades earlier, in 1918, he had retired from his position of professor of German culture and literature at Cambridge University in 1936. Two years later, he had been pressed into the British Intelligence Service because of his knowledge of Germany and the German people. As he had approached retirement in the mid-1930s, he had watched, first with interest, then with increasing concern, the rise of Hitler and Nazi Germany. Like Winston Churchill, he early on realized that this was a menace to Europe and ultimately to Great Britain.

For almost a month he had been debriefing members of the British Expeditionary Forces. Those who were being questioned had been plucked from the shores of France. From the beaches, protected by the temporary control of the overhead skies by the British air force, escaping capture or death by the German army, more than 330,000 had been plucked from the shores of France in a little over a week. Although of course he didn't know it, his son-in-law, William Lessing, whom he thought was long dead, was as Oberst Wilhelm Lessing at the same time in France also debriefing, or rather interrogating, members of the British Expeditionary

Forces—not those who had escaped and been returned to England, but those who had been captured by the German army.

Bradford was depressed for two reasons. First was the fact that the Germans now controlled most of Western Europe north of the Pyrenees. As he questioned the escapees from the beaches of Dunkirk and other French beaches and ports, he became increasingly aware of the desperate situation that Britain was in. Bereft of allies, she now stood alone against the master of Western, and probably soon to be all of, Europe.

His second concern was personal. He had just found out what had happened to his only grandson, Lieutenant Jacob Rosenstein. The lieutenant had been sent over the channel to help rescue one of the last groups of English soldiers still on the mainland. They were members of the British battalion that was fighting a holding rear-guard action as the remnants of the British Expeditionary Force were being rescued.

Bradford had been told that the orders for his grandson's squad, which itself had been rescued on the beach at Dunkirk a week or so earlier, were to return to the mainland, at Cherbourg. They were to wait for their arrival and make sure these soldiers, who had in their possession essential heavy equipment, were protected as they loaded the same small ship on which they were returning to France from the wharves of Cherbourg Harbor. The ship had arrived at Southampton, and Bradford was finally debriefing those members of the battalion who had also escaped just as the last ship was pulling away from the dock. His grandson was not one of them.

He was told that Lieutenant Rosenstein's squad of about ten men was at the barricade at the wharf's entrance as the ship was casting off. The firing from his group and that of the advancing Germans, neither of which had caused casualties, had ceased when the ship had been about five hundred yards removed from its mooring. The questioned sergeant didn't know the fate of the group. However, he did know that the lieutenant had been commanded to hold the line until the ship was safely away and that if escape then seemed improbable, he and his men should surrender rather than fight to the death against impossible odds. Better to live, to perhaps fight another day, than to die a martyr. Also, maintaining a captured prisoner would be a greater stress on the enemy.

He knew he had to relate this bad news to young Jacob's other grandfather. When the war had started, seventy-one-year-old William Lessing had been called out of retirement. With his years of experience in prewar Germany and France, he was serving as an adviser to Winston Churchill and other officials. Knowing such news should not be related over the telephone but in person, the next morning, July 2, 1940, Bradford walked the few blocks to Churchill's underground headquarters, passing the embassy of Spain on the way.

CHAPTER SEVENTEEN

LONDON, ENGLAND
JULY 2, 1940

The man who walked through the door was Lessing's father-in-law, James Bradford. As his father probably had already told him of his son's presence, his rather stern look in his son-in-law's direction was not one of surprise but of concern. Lessing's reaction was much different. He could not hold back his loud gasp as he sank down, not to the chair he had been sitting on, but to the top of his father's desk.

"Well, William, I believe your father and I are accepting that you are who you say you are," Bradford said. "You being here with your fantastic tale is an amazing occurrence. That the three of us are meeting makes it a remarkable happening, which is topped by the circumstance of your meeting with Jacob—that is, your William Jr. The question now is," he said as he walked over to his son-in-law, placing his arms around him, "what do we do now?"

"I'm not sure," Lessing said as he pulled away from his grasp. Buying time as his mind raced through the fantastic situation he now was in, he reached over and picked up the pitcher, filled a glass, and slowly drank the water from it.

"Let's see," his father said as he reached over for the pitcher. He poured his son another glass and repeated the operation for himself and James. "Let's calm down." He walked over to his desk and pulled his chair from behind it, placing it next to the one Lessing Jr. had been sitting on. He then plucked a third one from several that were around a table and placed it facing the other two. Another memory came rushing to the forefront of the son's mind. His father's placement of the chairs put the three of them on an equal footing, showing his years of experience as a diplomat.

Glancing at the clock on his desk and nodding toward his son, he continued, "It's still early in the day. Sit down. Tell us again what you told me so James can better know what the situation is." Another hour passed as the younger Lessing condensed what he had previously said, elaborating on what he thought were important facts.

When he finished, his father said, "Let's assume you are Solvanal, a Spanish diplomat, representing those Germans with a message for the prime minister, and let's review the situation. First, let's make the assumption that with Franco's knowledge, as a favor for the German, Admiral Canaris, you allow a German officer, posing as a minor Spanish diplomat, to arrange a meeting between them and the P.M. The purpose of your visit is to deliver a message, with the hope that a meeting between Canaris and appropriate officials of our government can be arranged. The objective of such a meeting is the arrangement of a truce between our two countries.

"Under that situation, James and I would go through the motions of contacting the prime minister to arrange a meeting with him. It is quite possible that he will refuse, because he would think that even talking to you could be seen as a weakness on his part. As for a truce with Germany, even if Hitler were gone, it would be unthinkable. In his mind, the only way to end the fighting is the unconditional surrender of Germany. Having gone through that charade, what is our next step?"

Pointing to his son, he said, "You, as you suggested, must go back to Gomez and tell him that after much sitting around and jockeying with secretaries, you finally got to see me and I arranged for you to meet with the P.M. tomorrow morning to deliver the admiral's message. As there quite possibly won't be such a meeting, the three of us will begin planning what advantage we can take of this amazing situation. And what to do about Jacob. First let us have lunch."

An hour or so later, he picked up the phone and said, "Will you arrange for transportation back to the Spanish embassy for Mr. Solvanal?" As Lessing Jr. left the room, he heard his father say, "James, let's see what our imaginations can develop to take advantage of this, our present, amazing situation."

James replied, "Yes, and Jacob."

"Of course," Lessing heard as the door closed behind him.

On the journey back to the embassy, Lessing mulled over his situation. Who was he really? His mind momentarily darted back to October 1918, when he woke up in the hospital and didn't know who he was. It was not the same now. At least who he was now was his decision. He was pretty sure his genes had made the decision for him. They were half American and half English. And that meant that he was a British soldier in this war. But he couldn't ignore the fact that for most of his adult life, he had been a German. At least he thought he was. His friends were German. Or was it "had been"? And it was a fact that his fellow soldiers for the last seven years were now his enemies.

Arriving back at the Spanish embassy, he was greeted by an anxious Gomez. He said he had been concerned when the hours passed and Lessing didn't return. He had been tempted to contact the British executive Lessing. (He didn't know that Canaris's agent was also a Lessing. He knew him only as a German posing as a Spaniard named Solvanal.) Lessing reassured him that the only problem had been the British bureaucracy, passing him from one secretary to another until he finally got to see Señor Lessing. Señor Lessing had said that he probably would be able to deliver his message to the prime minister the next morning.

CHAPTER EIGHTEEN

LONDON, ENGLAND

JULY 3, 1940

Lessing experienced a poor night's sleep, tossing and turning as again he mulled over the problem of his dual identities. He rose early and sat in a chair looking out the window that overlooked the approaching dawn as it relieved the blacked-out city of London with its early summer light. A knock on the door broke his reverie; looking at his watch he saw that it was eight o'clock. "Yes?" he said in Spanish. The reply was that there was a telephone call for him.

After hanging up the telephone, he followed the orderly to a small dining room, where he discovered he was very hungry. A thoughtful Gomez had arranged a typical German breakfast of cold meats, including their famous sausages, and cheeses served alongside a variety of breads and sweet toppings of jam, marmalade, and honey. These were followed by soft-boiled eggs and fruit, which rounded out the large, delicious breakfast.

By the time Lessing finished, he felt somewhat better, even though the meal had brought forward remembrances of his German identity. He was sitting at the second-floor window over the rather drab entrance to the reception hall of the Spanish embassy when the limousine with, he assumed, the senior Lessing in it pulled up at the embassy's Chesham Place entrance. As he looked down, the back door opened, and indeed it was him, arriving as the telephone call from him an hour earlier had scheduled, at nine o'clock.

Quickly hurrying down a stairway, Lessing arrived at the front entrance just as the door was being opened by the embassy's armed guard. As his father held out his hand, he greeted Lessing in Spanish as Solvanal, keeping the fiction, for Gomez's benefit, that the British believed Canaris's representative was a Spaniard.

"Buenas dias, Señor Solvanal. And to you also, Señor Ambassador."

He turned and held out his other hand to Gomez, who had come from his office, and then turned back to the younger Lessing. "The prime minister has given you some time after ten o'clock. If you will excuse us," he said to Gomez, "we should leave so that we get there at the appointed time to deliver Admiral Canaris's message."

In the backseat of the limousine he told his son that after he had left, he and James had spent a couple of hours discussing how they—meaning the British—could take advantage of his situation. In the end, they had a rough plan, which needed additional work to be developed into the final program. They had written a condensed summary of Lessing's situation and the basics of their plan, which they had sent by messenger to the prime minister.

At one hour after midnight, his father had been awakened by a call from Churchill's secretary, setting up the ten o'clock meeting. During the drive to the prime minister's headquarters, he told his son that he had not contacted his sister, Martha, nor his mother about her son, because the fact that Lessing was alive had to be kept in absolute secrecy. He had told them, however, that Jacob was alive but was a German prisoner.

When they arrived precisely at ten, only Lessing Sr. was invited into the prime minister's office. He had whispered into the secretary's ear as she escorted him from the outer office into the inner office. As for Lessing Jr., she gestured to a chair. She then talked to someone on her telephone. A few minutes later, a uniformed soldier entered the room with a pail of water, which he placed by Lessing's chair. His father had apparently asked the secretary to supply it, which she had done with a quizzical look on her face.

While Lessing was waiting, a dark-complexioned man, who appeared to be around forty years old, entered the outer office, glanced at Lessing, and was directed by the secretary to a door across the room from the P.M.'s. Lessing thought he looked vaguely familiar. Finally, as the minute hand on his watch hit six, the door to the prime minister's office opened and a young man appeared and invited him in. He picked up the pail and followed Lessing through the door.

Inside were Lessing's father, Prime Minister Winston Churchill, a middle-aged man whom the P.M. introduced as Colonel Thomas Robertson, and the young man, who was his secretary, John Coville. Surprisingly, the P.M., who was sitting behind his desk, was wearing a bathrobe over his pajamas. He rose and with a smile said, "William, your father has been telling me an amazing, almost unbelievable story about you. He has told me that your dual identity might be of great benefit to our country. Although it might seem that using your position as a high officer in Germany's Abwehr is a wonderful opportunity to spy, after discussing your situation with him, I have determined that we must be most careful in proceeding. Also I am sure you have a personal problem in resolving the conflict between your two identities. Therefore, I believe we should be, again I say, most careful how we proceed. I believe there is a better way than you serving as a direct spy.

"First, however, you must complete the mission that Admiral Canaris sent his Oberst here for. Your father has told me about the water pail procedure. Will you proceed to prepare the messages so that I can read them?"

"Yes, sir," Lessing replied.

He unbuttoned his coat and shirt, revealing the sealed envelope that was strapped to his stomach. Rolling up his shirt and coat sleeves, he put the envelope into the water and carefully opened it, removing the pieces of cloth from it while making sure that they remained under water. They were about five inches square and folded once. As he unfolded them into five-by-ten-inch sheets, writing began to appear. To his surprise, there were not two sheets but four. He recognized the admiral's handwritten messages on all of them.

The two additional sheets had something written on both sides. The two messages that he had translated into English for the admiral to copy had been returned to Lessing in the sealed envelope along with two additional sheets that he was unaware of! Oster had not told Lessing about them. There was complete silence for the next few minutes until he removed the sheets from the water and placed them on the towel that Coville had spread on the P.M.'s desk.

"Thank you, William," the P.M. said with a slight smile. "John, will you refresh William Sr.'s and Thomas's coffee? And pour one for Señor Solvanal." He sat down behind his desk and started reading the admiral's proposal.

Accepting the coffee, Lessing inwardly heaved a sigh of relief. The prime minister was not only a great leader, but also, as it was apparent that he realized Lessing's personal conflict, an understanding one.

For the next several minutes there was complete silence as he read the contents of the two sheets that Lessing had translated. Finally, laying those two sheets down and picking up one of the two additional sheets, he said, "Thomas, will you explain our plan for using William while I continue reading the admiral's proposals?"

CHAPTER NINETEEN

LONDON, ENGLAND

JULY 4, 1940

The two Lessings and Colonel Robertson retired to a small room where they sat around a table, upon which were a pot of coffee, some mugs, and small pastries. The colonel spoke. "What I am about to tell you is absolutely confidential. I mean absolutely, absolutely. Do you understand what I mean?"

Both of them nodded and answered in the affirmative.

"All right, first let me give you some history. Before the start of the war, as you are probably aware," he said, nodding to Lessing Jr., "the foreign branch of the German Abwehr recruited several people as spies here in Britain. These were people who for various reasons were anti-Britain. They agreed to provide their German handlers with information about the British armed forces, which they did until the war started. Then for all of them—I repeat, all of them—their love of country overcame any prewar anti-British feelings they had. As a result, all of them revealed to various responsible people here in England their role as a spy for Germany. And all of them agreed to become agents for us, becoming double agents."

Lessing was amazed. During his four years with Canaris his responsibilities had been in the Foreign Service Department of the

Abwehr, and he had not been involved in the Secret Intelligence Department except for gathering some minor information while he was in Spain. Then he remembered Juan Juhol. That was the man he had seen just a few minutes ago! He had appeared at the German embassy in Madrid just before Lessing had been called back by the admiral for the interrogation assignment. The admiral had already sent Major Pasht to replace him as the Abwehr agent in the Spanish capital. Johol had requested a meeting with the embassy's Abwehr agent. Lessing and the major had listened to him as he explained that he hated the communists, having fought against them in the civil war. He wanted to help the Führer fight them. He had a contact in England who could help him spy on England's communist party. As Lessing was leaving Spain, he had left him with the major to develop his task. And here he was in Churchill's war office!

Lessing interrupted Robertson. "Pardon me, Colonel. Isn't that Juan Juhol I just saw? Is he one of your 'double agents'?"

"Indeed he is. It turns out that although he hates communists, his detestation of Nazi fascism and Hitler have compelled him to help us. His German handler is Major Pasht.

"Now, here's what the prime minister would like you to do as an officer in the British army. At the present time many of the agents on both sides have individual handlers. We in the United Kingdom have created a central committee to oversee the handling of all the double agents. This committee is composed of representatives of all agencies in Britain that are involved in our war effort. Day-to-day handling of all the agents is by a much smaller group composed of some of the individual handlers and other people the day-to-day commander—that's me—deems appropriate." Robertston paused before asking, "Do either of you have questions?"

Father looked at son, who shook his head, saying, "Not now."

The colonel continued, "Now as to you, Colonel Lessing—yes, you," he said, looking at the shocked expression on Lessing's face, "the P.M. feels that what we are asking you to do warrants such a commission level. After all, if the Germans rank you at that level, so will we. You now will probably get colonel's pay in both deutsche marks and pounds," he said with a slight smile.

"Now, what we would like you to do: whereas our double agents are responsible generally here in Britain to the Committee of Twenty, in Germany each one has his own German handlers in the Abwehr Section 1. As you are aware, I'm sure, that section is under the control of Oberst Piekenbrock. However, the field agents have separate handlers; for instance, Johol has Major Pasht. We think they will work better if all of them in Germany report to a single master handler: you. We don't know what your relationship is with the admiral, only what you have related to your father." Nodding toward him, he said, "You must determine as soon as possible if you think you will be able to do this. The prime minister says that you can go back to Señor Gomez and tell him the prime minister will have an answer for you to take back to the admiral tomorrow morning. You can mull over the possibility of being able to do this and let us know tomorrow. Before we go back to the P.M., I have someone for you to talk to."

He got up, walked over, and opened the door. Juan Johol stepped in, stopping by the door. "The P.M. and I discussed this idea with Juan last night," the colonel said. "He thinks it is a good idea. This communication central helps prevent adverse actions by other British agents, doesn't it, Juan?"

Johol stepped farther into the room and sat down in the fourth chair at the table. Speaking with a slight Spanish accent, he replied, "Hello, Wilhelm—or should I say William?"

Not waiting for an answer, he continued, "One of our principal actions is supplying our German handlers—mine is Major Pasht—with fictitious information. Working with the committee allows us to avoid three problems. One, we can jointly reinforce each other's deceptive information. Second, we don't give our German handlers information that contradicts what others have given their handlers. And third, perhaps the most important, it reduces the chances of our true identities being revealed to the Germans. If we were to have a similar joint handler in Germany, we would have the protection of number three there."

There was a knock on the door, which then opened, and Coville stuck his head in and said, "The prime minister is ready for the three of you. Mr. Johol, if you will stay, Colonel Robertson will soon return." The three of them followed Coville to the P.M.'s office. He was now dressed in a suit and smoking a cigar. With a slight smile he stood up from his chair behind his desk and handed the younger Lessing an envelope, saying as he did so, "Señor Solvanal, I have written my reply to the admiral. It is in this sealed envelope. However," he said with a smile, "it is written in English, which you, not as the Spaniard Solvanal, but as Oberst Lessing, may want to translate into German if the admiral has trouble with my written English. So here," he said, picking up a sheet of paper, is a copy. The words are basically the ones I intend to say to Parliament tomorrow."

Lessing took the sheet and read the message to his father.

"'Admiral Canaris, I have received your message delivered by Señor Solvanol. I too would like to see the end of hostility between our two countries. But we don't have the slightest intention of entering into negotiations in any form and through any channel with the German and Italian governments. We shall, on the contrary, prosecute the war with the utmost vigor by all the means that are open to us.'"

"I shall deliver this to the admiral," Lessing said, opening his shirt and placing the envelope in the pouch of his belt.

"There is an additional subject in the envelope, one of which you probably are not aware," Churchill said. "In it I thank the admiral for revealing something that he probably thinks will sway me into calling a truce. And you, not as Solvanol, but as British Colonel Lessing, deserve to know what that is. He has given me an outline of Hitler's plan, called Sealion, for the invasion of our island. However, contrary to how he probably thinks, it actually gives us a plus. As the war continues and they try to invade us, this information of course will help us prepare appropriate defenses. We will discuss this further tomorrow morning."

He continued, "Now, as to the other matter. Your son, Jacob." He picked up the telephone on his desk and spoke a few words into it. As he hung it up, the door opened, and to Lessing's surprise, his father-in-law, James Bradford, joined them. The prime minister left, and for the next hour or so, both Lessings, father-in-law James, and Colonel Robertson discussed the implementation of the plan called "Fish Boat."

Fish Boat had two objectives. First would be developing a set of Britain's defense plans against Hitler's plan for the invasion of Britain, Sealion. They would appear to be plausible but would be fictitious, thereby possibly upsetting Hitler's plans. To get Canaris to accept them as plausible, Jacob's grandfather, a distressed James Bradford, would secretly deliver them, in exchange for Jacob's release. Which was the plan's second objective.

CHAPTER TWENTY

SCHWARZWALD (BLACK FOREST), GERMANY

JULY 5, 1940

Consciousness returned to Lessing again. This time he didn't have the severe pain in his head, only a mild headache. He opened his eyes. There, staring down at him, was Hilga! In German she said, "Ah, Oberst, you have rejoined us again. If you don't mind my saying so, this is getting to be a habit with you. Now that you are conscious, I'll get Hans—er, that is, Doctor Brachman." And she vanished.

Bewildered, realizing that he was lying in a bed, Lessing sat up without any particular effort. He was in a hospital again, in a room with two beds, the other one unoccupied. *What the hell happened to me?* he wondered. Suddenly he reached down and tore open the hospital gown he was wearing. The belt and envelope were still there! Heaving a sigh of relief, he tried to piece together what had happened. This time, thankfully, there was no memory problem. Glancing at his watch, he saw that it was a few minutes before twelve. Glancing up at a nearby window he saw that sunlight was shining through. Almost noon on the fifth, as he saw that the numeral 5 was peering out at him through the tiny date hole in the watch's face.

While waiting for Hans (Hans? Hilga? How was it possible?), Lessing reconstructed the past forty or so hours. He had not returned to stay at the Spanish embassy after the meeting with Churchill. His father had sent a messenger to Gomez to tell him that the British would fly him to Gibraltar immediately that day with Churchill's reply to Canaris. He had arranged for someone from the embassy to gather together his meager travel articles, which were picked up on the way to the airfield. Surprise.

And would the ambassador provide for someone to meet Señor Solvanol there and escort him to the German embassy in Madrid? Gomez had done so, and after several hours of flying and driving, Lessing had arrived there four hours after the sun had risen on the morning of July 4, two weeks and one day from the night that the falling beam changed his life forever.

And who of course had met him at the embassy? Julian! He had arranged for the 900-mile flight from Madrid to the Swiss capital, Bern. From there, after refueling, they would fly the 650 miles to Hamburg. The plane was a former Lufthansa four-passenger He 70 single-engine Heinkel, operated by his father's firm. After a short nap, Lessing ate lunch before the two of them, with Max the pilot, were on their way.

He now remembered what had happened—that is, up to a point. Three hours or so into the flight as they had approached some mountains, the airplane started to shake violently because of several updraft currents. Suddenly one of the auxiliary fuel tanks (one under each wing to increase the plane's range from 600 miles to 1,100) was shaken off, and the plane tipped to one side and dived down toward the ground. Max struggled with the controls to pull the plane out of its dive, but with little success. He finally was able to level out the dive somewhat and direct the descent to an open area, where the plane hit the ground and bounced. The next thing Lessing knew, he was in a hospital bed with nurse Hilga peering down at him.

As he reached that point of memory, she reappeared, accompanied by Doctor Hans. And Julian! And another nurse, much younger, who seemed to resemble someone in Lessing's mind, but who?

Lessing's thoughts were interrupted by Hans, who said, "This is unbelievable! For the third time you show up with a knock on the head."

At the same time, Julian was excitedly saying, "Thank God you are all right, Oberst. I have talked to General Oster on the telephone, and he has ordered me to bring Churchill's reply to him. That is, if you can't do it."

Lessing broke in. "Although I'm in a hospital, you appear to be all right. And Max? And Hans and Hilga!"

Hans started to reply, but Julian drowned him out. "Max was able to pretty much straighten the plane out before it hit the ground, so it just skidded over the uneven ground until it hit a tree. Fortunately we were belted in. Max and I were just shaken up. But your travel case fell off the overhead rack and hit you on the head. Because the crash site was only a few kilometers from Schonau and it wasn't quite dark yet, someone saw the crash, and within an hour you were here in the hospital. Amazingly, the chief doctor is Hans Brachman, who I found out has treated you before."

Lessing broke in again. "Hans and Hilga, what are you doing here? Aren't you with the Army Medical Division?"

Hans answered, "We are. However, with the fall of France, the fighting, at least for now, has essentially ceased. Because of our experience, we have been assigned to this hospital, which is treating more than a score of severely wounded soldiers. And by another remarkable coincidence, this is the hospital where Hilga and I have been treating patients for many years. Now, enough talking. Let's see if you can accompany Julian to Hamburg."

While the other three stood mutely by, he spent the next several minutes going through the medical examination routine with which Lessing was now quite familiar.

"There appears to be nothing really serious," he said. "However, because the bump on your head is in the exact location as your two previous problems, I would like to keep you here for another day, if possible."

With the last sentence being a question, Lessing felt he needed time to review his situation.

He replied, "I need to talk to Julian." Taking the hint, Hans left the room, beckoning to the two nurses to follow him.

Motioning Julian to come closer, Lessing said, "I am feeling rather woozy, and because the general is willing for you to deliver Churchill's reply, I'll take Hans's advice and give him another day." As he was saying that, he reached through the tear in the gown and removed the envelope and belt, which Julian accepted. Removing his shirt, he wrapped the belt around his body.

Continuing, he said, "When I get back, if the general and admiral so desire, I can give them my personal impression of the prime minister's attitude. However, as just the Spanish messenger Solvanal, I wasn't able to see the prime minister for more than a few minutes. I'm sure you will have no trouble finding a way to fly to Hamburg as soon as possible. And make a reservation for my return there tomorrow—or later if I must stay here longer."

As Julian left, the other three returned, Hilga carrying a tray with food on it. Hans spoke. "Here is your lunch. You should try to get some more sleep. We'll come back in a couple of hours." Lessing closed his eyes, and as he tried to think what his next moves should be, he dozed off. An hour or so later, he woke up when he sensed someone's presence. He opened his eyes, and there was Hilga standing by the bed. With her was the young nurse.

"Oberst," she said, her voice trembling. "I have something to tell you. The amazing coincidence that we have been reunited twice in the past few weeks compels me to tell you something that I have not told anyone else. It is personal, but I feel I must."

As she hesitated, it hit him. The bomb burst! Before she could continue, Lessing interjected, "This young lady." He pointed to the young nurse. "I presume she is our daughter."

Hilga gasped, collapsed on the chair beside the bed, and began crying. "Oh, Wilhelm, er, Oberst, how I wanted to tell you the other day. But I couldn't; after all, you are a senior officer and I'm just a nurse."

Before she could continue, he interjected again. "But you are an excellent head nurse, and as well, I'm sure, an excellent mother. Can you introduce me to our daughter? And to you I am Wilhelm, just as it was on that night so many years ago. And to her I am Father."

For the next half hour or so, the Lessing/Regensburg family of three brought their two families' histories up-to-date—mostly Hilga's and Wilhelmnina's, as bachelor Wilhelm Lessing was very careful about revealing the details of his life since that night so long ago. Finally, his headache returned in force, and Hilga recognized his discomfort, reached into her pocket, and pulled out a pill. When Lessing woke up in the early evening, he found that Hilga had arranged a family dinner with the two nurses and guest Hans, during which they revealed the father/daughter relationship to Hans. Lessing found that Julian had indeed provided for his journey home. He was in Hamburg by early afternoon the next day after a dramatic family farewell, the drive to the nearest airstrip, and the 300-mile, two-hour flight.

CHAPTER TWENTY-ONE

ABWEHR HEADQUARTERS
JULY 6, 1940

Upon landing, Lessing was met by a car and driver, who quickly took him to Abwehr headquarters. He was met by Julian, who silently greeted him and hastily escorted him to the admiral's office.

There Admiral Canaris and Majorgeneral Oster were waiting for him. After some questions and answers about his head problem (there was still a patch over the point of impact), the admiral got to the point of the meeting. Did Churchill really mean, "If no surrender, no meeting"?

Lessing explained that as the Spaniard Solvanal, he was just the messenger, so he hadn't gotten much time with the prime minister. However, his impression was that the prime minister was serious when he had handed him the envelope and muttered "Unconditional."

"Damn," said Canaris. Then to Lessing, he said, "Well, we tried. Take a couple of days off, get some rest, and then report to the general." He nodded toward Oster.

"Wait," Lessing said as he began the subterfuge code-named Fish Boat that had been agreed upon in London two days earlier. "I have something to suggest to you. I believe that the trip wasn't a complete failure. While I was waiting in the prime minister's outer office, Juan Juhol passed through. When he saw me, his jaw dropped in astonishment. Fortunately, the secretary had already noticed him and her head was turned back to her desk by then, so she didn't see it."

The admiral broke in. "Wait a minute. Who is this Juhol?"

"He is Major Pasht's agent. I met him at our embassy in Madrid several months ago. When he saw me, he quickly recovered and made a slight nod at me and left the room by a side door. I was as astonished as he apparently was."

Having answered the admiral's question, Lessing continued: "To continue, sir, the prime minister suggested that I leave on my return to Germany with his replies as soon as possible. He offered to arrange for me to fly back to Gibraltar that evening. As Solvanal, I accepted his offer, so he ordered a senior member of his staff, a James Bradford, to make the arrangements.

"While he was doing this, Mr. Churchill handed me the envelope containing his answer to you.

"About half hour or so later, James Bradford returned and led me to an underground garage and a large shiny black sedan with a civilian driver. And of all people beside him in the front seat, there was Juan Juhol!

"As I have already told you, Juhol had glanced at me and nodded as he passed through the door out of the prime minister's office reception room, which I understood meant that he wanted to talk to me. With Bradford and the British driver in the car, what Juhol and I said to each other was quite neutral, leaving anything else for our ears only, until we were alone. Therefore, on the drive to the landing field, we were quite quiet. But James Bradford, who had joined me in the rear seat, was not."

The admiral broke in. "What do you mean, this James Bradford was not? What did he say?"

"Although he didn't know it, he related an amazing coincidence to me. During the hour or so drive to the airfield to catch the airplane to Gibraltar, the James Bradford who had provided the automobile, I found out, was the grandfather of a captured British lieutenant Manz and I had interrogated in Cherbourg a few weeks ago. Because he thought that Juhol was a British agent and that I, as Solvanal, was a neutral Spaniard, he was not careful about what he said. He sorrowfully related the story about a Jacob Rosenstein, his grandson, who is now a prisoner of war being held by the Germans (that is us) with the middle names William Lessing. He was fearful that with the Jewish name Rosenstein, he might not be treated according to the Geneva code for prisoners."

The Admiral and the General appeared somewhat entranced by what Lessing was relating to them. After asking for and getting a drink of water that a sailor brought in, he continued.

"When we arrived at the airfield, Bradford started to talk to the driver as Juhol and I walked from the car to the isolated loading area for the airplane. Juhol explained to me that he was our double agent. Juhol had told his British handler, a Colonel Robertson, whom he was going to meet when I saw him go through the door in the prime minister's office, that one of his French contacts had definitive information about the French fleet defeat at Oran. And he had to get back to the continent as soon as possible to get this information. What he really needed to do first, of course, was tell me what he was doing in the British prime minister's office.

"So he joined me in the airplane for the 900-mile, five-hour flight to Gibraltar. The plane had accommodations for four passengers and two pilots. However, because there was only one pilot, I secretly ordered Juhol to sit with the pilot. I did this because as Bradford, who was sitting with me in the passenger compartment—"

The Admiral broke in again, "Bradford joined you on the airplane?"

"Yes," Lessing said before he continued relating to the admiral and general what had then happened. "As the airplane's refueling was still going on, I returned alone to the car and asked Bradford to join me in walking out to the boarding area. Walking slowly, I told him that what I was about to say was just between the two of us. That if he wanted to ever see his grandson again, he would remember that. And I suggested that he join me on the flight to Gibraltar.

"Stunned, he was silent until we got on the plane, where he agreed to keep our conversation private. With Juhol in the cockpit with the pilot and the roar of the engines, Bradford's and my conversation was private. I told him that I was not a Spaniard acting as a messenger for Admiral Canaris but a German Oberst under Admiral Canaris. That as an interrogator of prisoners, I had interrogated his grandson and that my name is Wilhelm Lessing. That it was possible that we were related in some way. That because Manz was a member of the SS, I also was concerned about the Jewish name. And that the admiral had the same concern about the mistreatment of Jews."

Lessing continued the tale, telling the two of them that he had then taken a giant leap. That he had proposed to Bradford after they got on the airplane that it was possible that Abwehr could get his grandson released if he could get certain information for them. Specifically, how Churchill had reacted to the information about Sealion.

Again Canaris broke in. "How did you learn that about Sealion? Did Churchill tell you?"

"No—Puhol told me. His British handler, Robertston, had told him, instructing him to get as much information as he could from his contacts over here."

The admiral said, "All right; continue."

Continuing his narrative, Lessing told the admiral he had assured Bradford that he could get the admiral to honor an agreement with essentially the following conditions.

1. Your agreement, as Admiral Canaris, with Bradford would be known only to yourself, your chief of staff, Majorgeneral Oster, and myself, Oberst Lessing.
2. That you would restrict his assignment to only a detailed analysis of Britain's reaction to Hitler's Sealion.
3. Bradford's analysis would be written in his hand. When it was completed, he would find a way to get it secretly to Spain's ruler, Francisco Franco, who I was sure would agree to be the intermediary between you and the British. Said delivery would end your association with him.

4. That you as the head of the Abwehr would take the necessary
   steps to secure the release of Jacob W. L. Rosenstein from
   German custody."

Finishing the fabricated recital, Lessing recommended to the admiral that he replace Major Pasht as Puhol's handler. He told them that this was because of a possibility of getting him to keep an eye on the operation. Lessing then continued his tale, finishing with a question to the admiral. "What do you think of my plan? Do you have any questions?"

"I do and I'm sure the general does also," Canaris said. "However, we'll wait until tomorrow to ask them." He reached into a drawer in his desk and pulled out an envelope and several sheets of paper. "Write a summary of what you have just told us. Seal it in this envelope and place it in this drawer. The general and I have a lot to talk about. We will think about it tonight and discuss it in the morning. You be here at noon." Lessing completed the summary, and because it was a warm evening, he chose to walk back to his quarters. While passing the visitors' quarters where Manz had stayed, he noticed that there was a light in that room's window. *Is he still there?* he wondered.

Before he retired, in his mind, Lessing reviewed Fish Boat. First: He had given Canaris and Oster the fabricated story of his meeting with Juhol. Second: He had recommended to the admiral that he replace Major Pasht as Puhol's handler. He told them that this was because of a possibility of getting control of a member of Churchill's senior staff. This was taking advantage of the amazing coincidences that James Bradford was the grandfather of the British lieutenant, with the Jewish name Rosenstein, whom he and Manz had interrogated in Cherbourg a few weeks ago. He said that he had told Bradford that he was not a Spaniard acting as a messenger for Admiral Canaris but a German Oberst under Admiral Canaris who had interrogated his grandson and that his name was Wilhelm Lessing. He had said it was possible that they were related. Lessing spent a half hour or so summarizing his fiction to them, including the fiction that Bradford had joined Lessing and Juhol on the flight to Gibraltar because he wanted more detail on what he had to do, if he agreed. When he had finished, at Canaris's order he had handwritten the summary.

CHAPTER TWENTY-TWO

REVIEW

What had actually happened during the previous forty-eight hours was, of course, different from the tale Lessing had told the admiral and the general. As he had learned from Robertson, Juan Juhol was one of the double agents that he had talked about. Although it appeared to the Germans that he was their double agent, he was actually working for the British and did need the information about the defeat of the French fleet at Oran, so that he could prepare a true report for the British and a slightly warped one for his German handler, Pasht. The latter would almost be correct, but with errors that in the long run would probably confuse the German navy. He therefore took advantage of Lessing's flight to Gibraltar, joining him in the Auro for the flight to Gibraltar. And contrary to what he had related, James Bradford did not.

During the five-hour flight, with Juhol sitting with Lessing, they had reviewed, slightly modifying and planning the implementation of Fish Boat.

First, James Bradford was to prepare the fictional analysis of the reaction of Churchill and his military commanders, with their help, to the outline of Sealion that he (unknowingly) had delivered to Churchill for Admiral Canaris. The analysis would be essentially pure fiction, but one that Canaris's analyzers would consider plausible.

Second, Winston Churchill had asked Robertson to help Lessing, his father, and father-in-law develop a plan for gaining the release of his son, Jacob, with the provision that the risk for Britain would be minimal.

Within an hour they, with Lessing being primarily only a spectator, had finalized the plan the two of them had developed the previous day. It involved Jacob's grandfather James Bradford. The story that Lessing would relate to the admiral, would be that Bradford was distraught upon finding that his only grandson was a prisoner of the Germans. His concern was increased by his knowledge of the potential fate of the Jews in Germany. Although he knew that Jacob, even though he had the final name Rosenstein, wasn't a Jew, his last name would probably cause his captors to think he was.

Therefore, the plan, bearing the title suggested by Churchill, Fish Boat, was that Oberst Lessing would relate to Canaris that on the one-hour drive to the British airfield, Bradford, thinking that Lessing was the neutral Spaniard Sovanal, broke down and related his concern.

Lessing would tell the admiral that he saw this as a possible chance to get some important British secrets. So he then had confessed to Bradford that he was not a Spaniard but a German Oberst on Admiral Canaris's staff, and that he could arrange for the release of his grandson if he would give him the British reaction to the information on Sealion that the admiral had given to the British prime minister.

Lessing's implementation of Fish Boat would continue as he told the admiral and Oster that when Bradford heard that, he said he would like time to consider what to do; that when they got to Gibraltar, he had said he was willing to provide the information; and that he would meet with Lessing at the Spanish embassy in Lisbon in two weeks or so—say, July 22. He would deliver his report if Lessing had his grandson with him.

It had been a busy and mentally exhausting day, but satisfying. If Canaris approved the plan, Jacob would soon be home. As Lessing drifted off to sleep, there was a smile on his face. After all, the admiral was one of the most powerful men in Germany. It should be a breeze. And oddly, he was beginning to enjoy his double life. It was like a big game. And no one was really getting hurt ... How wrong he was.

.

CHAPTER TWENTY-THREE

GERMANY

JULY 7, 1940

Sleeping in until almost 0730, Lessing ate a quick breakfast in the officers' dining hall and spent the next four hours going through various documents and making contacts to find out where the sergeant, Josef Schmidt, was. At 10:13, he was rewarded. Schmidt was actually on leave in Hamburg. Lessing contacted him and ordered him to meet him at the admiral's office at noon. Together they entered Canaris's office at twelve o'clock.

Lessing was surprised to see that in addition to Majorgeneral Oster, Julian was there, as was Oberst Piekinbrock, head of the Abwehr secret intelligence section, and Oberst Von Bentivegri, head of the Abwehr counterespionage section. Seeing the look of surprise on his face, the admiral hurried over to Lessing and asked him to go with him as he walked to a corner of his office where there was a watercooler.

"The two Obersts know nothing about the real reason about Bradford," the admiral said. "The general and I will discuss that with you later; this is only about his grandson. We have to convince everyone who is involved in any way with our agent program that the lieutenant needs to be found and convinced that he should become our agent. When this is done, we will have a valid reason for getting him to England, thereby meeting our part of the agreement with Bradford, which only the three of us and Julian and Juhol know about."

Going to the chair behind his desk, he gestured for the five of them to stand at ease before his desk. Nodding toward Julian and the two Obersts, he said, "I want you three to assist Oberst Lessing in an operation that has possibilities of reaping important information about the British. Several weeks ago, Oberst Lessing was interrogating captured British soldiers. One, by a remarkable coincidence, had the same last name as the Oberst: Lessing.

"Intrigued by this, I asked General Oster to do some research. He has come up with some interesting information. If you will join him in his office, he will relate it to you."

Lessing, General Oster, the two Obersts, and Julian all saluted the admiral (with the usual military salute, not the one accompanying "Heil Hitler") and followed the general out the door and into his office, which was adjacent to that of the admiral.

That morning he and Julian had dreamed up a fantastic program, one they thought would convince everyone involved in Abwehr espionage. It was the development of a superspy for the Abwehr. (They didn't know it, but the program would be one of the two integral parts of Fish Boat: the return of Lessing's son to England.)

When they were all seated, the general began. "I asked Oberleutnant Fuerst to do some research. Julian, tell them what you found out."

The lieutenant rose and said, "The Englishman who was captured a couple of weeks ago in Cherbourg and the Oberst very possibly might have the same ancestor, a German named Max Lessing. This Lessing had moved from Prussia to South Africa in the latter part of the nineteenth century. He married the daughter of a minor Prussian diplomat, who was stationed in Cape Town. They had several sons. He was involved in the First Boer War with England, and apparently was captured and taken to England around 1880 and imprisoned. When the war was over, he was released. However, he didn't return to South Africa. His wife's father had been transferred to England,

and she and their sons joined her father in London when Lessing was imprisoned there. When he was released, the family remained in London. As the sons reached adulthood, some of them migrated to Prussia. They would have been in their early twenties. Their oldest sons, the grandsons of Max, were in World War One. One of these sons could be the Oberst."

Noticing the startled looks on the Oberst's and sergeant's faces, the lieutenant diverted from his recital. "You are unaware that the Oberst has what is called autobiographical amnesia. He has no recollection of his life before he was seriously wounded in the First World War. Other than the name Lessing on the back of the Knights Cross around his neck, there were no clues about his life before he was wounded."

Returning to his recital, he continued. "I found the records of four Lessings in the war. However, none of them seemed to have come close to the education that the Oberst has. As to the English lieutenant, he quite possibly is a great-grandson of the South African Lessing, which means that possibly he is a nephew, once or twice removed, of the Oberst. I found the record of a William Lessing, a son of one of the Prussian migrants, who was born in 1918 in England, apparently during a visit by his mother to his English relatives. He apparently returned to Prussia with his mother, living there until his parents were killed in an automobile accident in 1933, when he was about fifteen. For some reason, rather than living with his German relative, he was returned to England—possibly because he was born there. I couldn't find any more information about him."

"But I did," the general spoke up. "In England, a Juan Puhol, who is one of our double agents, found something that adds to what the lieutenant has told you. A few days ago, this Juhol happened to overhear a loud conversation between two senior English officials while he was waiting for contact with his English handler. One of the Englishmen was named Rosenstein, and the other one had just told him that his—that is Rosenstein's—adopted son, Jacob, had been captured by our army.

"I am paraphrasing Rosenstein's reply: 'He's not my son. As far as I'm concerned, if one of our officers becomes a war prisoner, let it be him rather than someone else. He was nothing but a pain in the neck ever since he was returned to us in 1933. But Sarah insisted that because he was the son of one of her brothers, we had to adopt him. For the next five years until he enlisted in the army, my life at home was a living hell. Sarah's life probably was as well. Fortunately, my duties required me to travel quite a bit. He insisted on speaking only German, not only at home but with the neighbors and relatives. And he had to be, literally, almost dragged to services at the synagogue. Because of the language problem, we had to send him to a private school. Fortunately, to my relief he was drafted. Oddly, in spite of his problems, he apparently was well educated, for the army gave him a commission.'

"Now," Oster concluded, "the Oberst has some comments."

Lessing had been admiring the tale of fiction that the general and Julian had concocted, so he hesitated, reaching over and pouring a glass of water from a pitcher on a nearby table, drinking it as his mind raced. "What you have revealed explains a lot," he finally said.

"He answered our questions in German," he continued. "At the time we thought he was taunting us. But now I believe that he was almost glad to be back in a German-speaking country. As I recollect, he didn't seem too distressed about being captured. Did you get that impression, Schmidt?" Lessing said in a strong voice, looking directly at him.

Schmidt didn't answer immediately.

"Well?"

"I guess so," he finally said.

"All right," Oster said. "It is possible we can develop this British soldier into a valuable agent. He obviously has a liking for the German language, and quite possibly an anti-Jewish attitude. We need to get ahold of him. Find this Lessing with the last name Rosenstein and bring him here," he said, looking at Lessing.

CHAPTER TWENTY-FOUR

CHERBOURG AND BEYOND

JUNE 18–19, 1940

As the darkness of one of the year's longest days finally descended on the town, whose streetlights were not working, German soldiers quickly appeared carrying torches, which kept the darkness from enveloping the town's main street. Lieutenant William Rosenstein, now a prisoner of war, struggled to keep up with the escorting German soldiers. Probably because their Oberst had shown respect for their prisoner, they did as well, actually supporting him as they rapidly strode down the street to the city's town hall. Even though there was a rather large group of prisoners there, there was no confusion as they entered the main hall. All the prisoners, who had spent the last several days practically running from the advancing motorized Wehrmacht, were sitting on the floor, stripped of all their belongings down to the clothes on their backs.

As he reached the hall, Manz left the escorts, heading back to the inn. The sergeant, with the notebook under his arm, entered the hall's office, joining three other noncommissioned officers. The two guards pushed Lessing into the small group of English prisoners, who, with only a little urging by their guards, had separated themselves from the rest of the captured soldiers. Perhaps because of their relatively casualty-free victory, their captors were treating them with a degree of kindness as they sat on the floor, eagerly eating the hash of vegetables and meat given to them.

Rosenstein also wolfed down the hash in the bowl handed to him by one of the other prisoners. As his hunger abated, he started to review the day's happenings in his mind.

First was the successful escape of the boat with the two tanks and several trucks along with their crews. Second was the capture of him and his squad by the Germans. Third was his interrogation by the German major in his stilted English. "All right, let's begin. What is your name and …"

He recalled that when he answered, his name seemed to invoke a strong reaction from the German colonel—or Oberst, they were calling him—and that his name was remarkably similar to his own and, for that matter, his father's. And there was a facial resemblance to his grandfather. Could there be … ? *Nonsense,* he thought. *I have a real problem. What is going to happen to us?* As he started to mull over this question in his mind, the long day's stress took over, and he curled up alongside the members of his squad and was asleep within minutes.

He was rousted up by his captors a couple of hours later when a train pulling two boxcars on the tracks across the street from the town hall arrived. He, along with all the other captured soldiers, was loaded onto one of the cars.

Lieutenant Rosenstein, along with the sergeant and the twelve privates under his command and a couple of dozen or so other British and French soldiers, all prisoners of war, sat on the floor of a small French boxcar, his back against one of the car's walls. The boxcar was swaying back and forth as it, the train's other boxcar, and a passenger car occupied by German soldiers were pulled northward toward Belgium. Unbeknownst to him, the sergeant who had been part of the Oberst Lessing and Major Manz interrogation team was also on the train.

As the train started to pick up speed, those inside the boxcar suddenly crouched down as they heard the familiar sounds of a dropping bomb along with the roar of an airplane coming from somewhere nearby. Rosenstein clenched his fists, waiting for the explosion, which never came; there was only the sound of splitting wood.

For several hours, the train's journey was punctuated by lurching stops and jerking starts as additional boxcars were added. During some of the stops, the door was opened and the prisoners were allowed to get out and, with the four soldiers watching, relieve themselves. One of the stops in the early morning light was at a small village where a Frenchman, overseen by two German soldiers, supplied them with water and bread. Prisoners from the other cars were kept isolated in individual groups by their guards.

The car's swaying, his fatigue, the blackness, the train stopping several minutes after starting, the addition of more prisoners, the four German soldiers leaving and closing and locking the car's door behind them, causing complete darkness, and the humid heat caused by the sweat of the prisoners all tended to dull Rosenstein's mind. There was an almost complete eerie silence in the car as each of the prisoners, with only a few words to a fellow captive, contemplated his plight. Ahead lay the unknown. For all intents and purposes, was his life over?

As Rosenstein drifted in and out of sleep, he mused over the fact that the Oberst had essentially the same name as his father. Was it just a remarkable coincidence or something of greater significance, and if it was the latter, what did it mean?

Hours later, he was jerked awake for seemingly the hundredth time by the sound of the car's door being pulled open and the sergeant, who in his accented voice shouted out, "End of line—all out." Rosenstein recognized him as the same soldier who been in the interrogation room. looked at his watch: 1700 hours. They had been on the train for almost a complete day. As the same four soldiers herded the car's captives into a loose marching formation which was joined by similar formations of prisoners from the train's other cars, Rosenstein looked around. The train had stopped at a siding in an area that seemed isolated except for what appeared to be—what? *A prison, perhaps?* he thought. No, it was too nonfortress-like.

Of course: a prisoner-of-war compound! In front of them were gates in two high barbed-wire fences, about twenty feet apart. They ran parallel to each other, appearing to be several hundred feet long. Both were about ten feet high. At each end, between the fences, was a wooden tower. In them he could see that each was manned by three soldiers, armed with rifles and a machine gun. Although he couldn't see them, he was sure that there were other fences surrounding the many wooden buildings inside. Judging by the appearance of their unpainted wood walls, they appeared to have recently been constructed. Yes, indeed, a prisoner-of-war camp.

As he and the others were marched through the gates, he saw a few men—prisoners, he reasoned—standing in the shade of one of the buildings, staring at the new arrivals. The march ended at a large open area, seemingly in the center of the camp, paved with a gravel-like stone. The sergeant standing next to Rosenstein, shouted, "Sit down. Not you," he added in a low voice as he grasped Rosestein by the right elbow and led him past the other prisoners, toward one of the smaller buildings.

Rosenstein was startled. "What's happening? Where are you taking me?"

Surprisingly, probably because of the special interest the Oberst had shown for this prisoner the day before, the German answered in his stilted English, "This is the Durchgangslager, where prisoners are asked for their name and rank so that they can be sent to the proper camps. Because you gave Major Manz that information yesterday, you don't have to go with the rest."

"Thank you," Rosenstein said. Another name—Major Manz—to go with Oberst Lessing. He wondered if the answer was that simple as the sergeant opened the door and pushed him into the building.

CHAPTER TWENTY-FIVE

ABWEHR HEADQUARTERS
JULY 7, 1940

After eating a delayed lunch, in Oster's office, the general, Lessing, Schmidt, Julian, and the two Obersts, began developing the plan to find Jacob and go through the ruse of attempting to turn him from a British agent into an undercover agent for Germany. The admiral's basic plan, that was recommended to him by Lessing, was to get a copy of England's defense plan against Hitler's Sealion. However the basic plan, unknown by the admiral, was not his but England's. The real reason, unknown by any of the Germans, was implementation of Churchill's plan Fish Boat, to deceive the Germans on England's plan to defeat Hitler's invasion of England and to free Jacob from captivity.

An example of Wilhelm against Winston, in the same package as Winston against Wilhelm.

The first thing was to find out where Rosenstein was. This task was given to the Sergeant Josef Schmidt, who had been allowed to join the planning group. After eating, he was given a document, signed by the admiral, giving him the authority needed for his search. Lessing started by asking what his actions with the prisoner were after they had left the inn in Cherbourg where the interrogation had taken place. Schmidt explained the procedure that was used to get the group of prisoners by train to the captured-prisoner compound, which was in Belgium. There the usual registering of captured enemy soldiers occurred before they were delivered to various POW camps: Stalags and Oflags. As Rosenstein had already been entered into POW records, he was separated from his fellow captured soldiers and treated differently.

"I had orders to deliver Rosenstein to Lieutenant Colonel Brummeir of the SS subunit in Berlin," Schmidt said.

Alarmed, Lessing interrupted his discourse. "What do you mean? Who gave you that order? I was your commanding officer at the time."

Schmidt hesitated.

"Answer me!" Lessing almost shouted.

"You were in the hospital at the time. Major Manz gave the order."

The other group members kept silent as Lessing calmed down and continued. "What happened then?"

"The major told me that his orders were to deliver Rosenstein to a specific location. Where, he could not tell me. And he didn't. After I delivered him to Brummeir, they left the room with the prisoner by a back door, with no more comment, and that is the last I saw of either one of them."

There was a complete silence as all looked at Lessing. "Do any of you have any comment or questions?"

The three of them shook their heads.

"All right, Sergeant Schmidt, on your way. Find him as soon as possible. When you do, report to me and I will call our group together again."

CHAPTER TWENTY-SIX

ABWEHR HEADQUARTERS

JULY 8, 1940

Lessing spent the next day and most of the second day trying to implement Robertston's One Major Handler plan. First Lessing got the admiral to set up a meeting between himself, Oberst Piekinbrock, and the admiral to discuss such an agent control system. The Oberst, acting somewhat like a bureaucrat, was reluctant to change. However, with a bit of nudging by the admiral, he agreed to work with Lessing on the possibility of such a change. The first step was to secure the names of the Abwehr agents.

On the afternoon of the second day, the collection process was interrupted by Sergeant Schmidt. He had eagerly appeared in the admiral's outer office asking—in fact, almost demanding—that he be permitted to report to Oberst Lessing. A few minutes later, he was in Oster's office, where the general and Lessing heard a most intriguing tale.

After accepting and drinking a cup of coffee, Schmidt began his report.

His search had begun in Berlin, looking into the activities of Manz, who was a member of the same SS subunit as its commander, Lieutenant Colonel Brummeir. Brummeir was the officer to whom Schmidt had delivered Rosenstein, per Manz's order. Fortunately,

Schmidt had a longtime friend in the subunit, a Sargentmajor Pacher—whose commander, by an amazing coincidence, was Lieutenant Colonel Brummeir. It seems that his friend Sargentmajor Pacher hated his commander for many reasons, one of which was making him, a sargentmajor, his driver. He told Schmidt that he had been the driver of the auto that took Rosenstein to Brussels as a prisoner of war.

Inviting his friend out to dinner at a fancy restaurant, Schmidt got some interesting information.

In March, Himmler's number-two man, Obergruppenführer Heydrich, had appeared at SS headquarters. The substance of Schmidt's tale was that Heydrich had told Brummeir and Manz that the Führer had ordered Admiral Canaris to develop a program that, following the army's advance into the Netherlands, Belgium, and France, would involve the interrogation of captured Allied soldiers.

Canaris had done so, selecting an Oberst named Wilhelm Lessing as the head. When informed about the program, Reichführer Himmler had suggested to the Führer that someone from the SS should be part of the interrogation team.

Schmidt continued with the condensed version of his story, saying Hitler had agreed and Manz had been selected to join Lessing. The day before Manz left for Hamburg to join Lessing, he had appeared with Obergruppenführer Heydrich, and Pacher had escorted them into Brummeir's office—another reason he hated Brummeir for making him his secretary.

Pacher had been sitting at his desk when Himmler and Manz arrived. His interest aroused, he clicked on the recording device that he had secretly installed in Brummeir's office, hoping to get some incriminating information that he could use against him.

Having told Lessing this, Schmidt reached into his pocket and pulled out a tape, which he handed to him. Making sure that all doors were closed, Lessing placed the tape into a playback machine. Putting on his earphones, he heard the following conversation.

Heydrich's voice said, "While I expect you, Major Manz, to do your best to work with Oberst Lessing to see that the Führer's program is efficiently carried out, this might give us an opportunity for a personal plus: a chance to get something on that traitor Canaris."

Brummeir's voice replied, "I agree. And the major is the man for the job. He has learned to speak rather good English and a bit of French. His experience at the Munich library of dealing with people can help in his dealing with prisoners. After all, we must follow the Geneva Convention rules. In so doing, you, Major, will not alert Canaris's man, this Lessing, that you have not only the responsibility of getting appropriate information from the captured prisoners but a second responsibility for the German people: routing out traitors. And a third: keeping a record of those prisoners with unseeingly names and backgrounds."

Brummeir's voice continued. "This Lessing interests me. Autobiographical amnesia for two decades! Just doesn't smell right."

Heydrich echoed that comment. "I agree. But other than the amnesia thing and the fact that he is under Canaris, he has an outstanding record, for a non-SS man." He added, "Keep an eye on him, Major."

There was nothing of additional significance on the tape for the next several minutes. After three "Heil Hitlers," the tape ended.

As Lessing started to remove the earphones, Schmidt reached into his pocket and pulled out another tape. Lieutenant Colonel Brummeir had had Pacher place a call to Obergruppen Heydrich, and Pacher had recorded the call on June 19.

Brummeir's voice said, "Heil Hitler! Obergruppenführer, I have some interesting information about Manz's actions with Lessing."

Heydrich's voice said, "I've just learned that Lessing has been badly injured. Do you have the details?"

"Yes, Obergruppenführer," Brummeir replied. "I have just received a coded message from Major Manz. Here is a condensed version of his tale. Yesterday a Stuka bomb accidentally fell on the inn where the Oberst and Major Manz were finishing their interrogation program. Fortunately, it didn't explode, but it did fall through the building's roof, and a wooden beam apparently hit Oberst Lessing on the head. He has just become conscious, and the doctor doesn't think he is too badly hurt. But an interesting development has occurred. The last prisoner they interrogated was a British lieutenant named Jacob Rosenstein." Lessing heard a kind of grunt, possibly from Heydrich.

Brummeir's voice continued, "Yes, an interesting detail. But the interesting point is he said his middle names—that's right, names plural—were William Lessing! Manz had been doing the questioning. The Oberst was in an adjacent room, and when Rosenstein said, 'William Lessing,' he came to the room's door. Manz said he seemed very interested and questioned the prisoner about having two middle names. The prisoner said they were his father's, who had been killed in the last war. When asked about the name Rosenstein, he said his mother had died at his birth and that he had been adopted by his father's sister, who had married a Jacob Rosenstein. An—" He was interrupted by Heydrich.

"An interesting tale," Heydrich said. "Where is Manz now?"

"He is in Cherbourg," Brummeir said, "compiling the details of the interrogation program. He said that he and Oberst Lessing will fly to Hamburg as soon as Lessing is able. As to Rosenstein, he is on a prisoner train with the other members of his detail on its way to a Durchgangslager in Belgium. That's all that Manz told me."

There was a kind of humming sound for a minute or so, and then Heydrich's voice returned.

"You pick up Rosenstein at the Durchgangslager. I'll develop a plan for him and wire it to you there. Heil Hitler!"

"Heil Hitler! Herr Obergruppenführer!" There was the sound of telephones hanging up, and then silence.

Lessing contemplated what he had heard for several minutes. Schmidt broke the silence. "Pacher told me that he and Brummeir left an hour or so later and flew to Brussels, where they picked up a sedan and drove south to the Durchgangslager, arriving a couple of hours before I arrived with the lieutenant. They then drove him to Stalag Saint-Gilles in Brussels. And that's all Pacher could tell me. After dropping Rosenstein off, they returned the sedan and flew back to Berlin."

CHAPTER TWENTY-SEVEN

STALAG SAINT-GILLES, BRUSSELS
JUNE 20–JULY 10, 1940

"Heil Hitler. Oberstleutenant, here is the prisoner I was ordered to deliver to you."

Returning Sergeant Schmidt's salute, Oberstleutenant Brummeir growled, "It's about time. My driver and I have been waiting for hours."

Grasping the left elbow of Lieutenant Jacob William Lessing Rosenstein, and opening an outside door, he muttered in English, "Come on" and led his prisoner to a parked black Citroen sedan. Pushing Rosenstein into the backseat, he joined the vehicle's driver in the front. As he settled down, he flicked a switch that locked the rear doors.

Rosenstein asked, "Where are you taking me?"

Brummeir replied, "Never mind. You'll find out soon enough. Just be quiet."

For the next several hours the sedan with its three passengers headed north toward Brussels. A steady stream of various types of military vehicles passed them going the other way. From time to time the driver had to pull off the road to allow room for large tanks to pass by. Around noon they pulled into an area with a group of a dozen or so trucks. One was a mobile kitchen from which the driver got three boxes of food and bottles of water.

Late in the afternoon, the car reached Brussels, and Stalag Saint-Gilles soon loomed up before them. A state prison before the war, it had been taken over by the Geheime Feldpolizei, the German military police. It was three stories high with five wings radiating from a central round core.

Opening the sedan's rear-seat door, Brummeir ordered Rosenstein to get out. Again grasping Rosenstein by the elbow, he walked him through the massive timber gates into the building. Inside was a courtyard with each of the five wings having a cast-iron gallery rising from it in tiers. Half an hour later, Rosenstein was sitting on a steel cot, in a small cell on the third floor, eating cooked cabbage.

For ten days and nights of semi-isolation, he was allowed an hour each day in a small fenced outside area. Each day there would be several other prisoners, none of them British. The other twenty-three hours he was alone in the isolation cell. On June 30, as the early summer sun began to shine through the cell's small window, he was wakened by a guard, fed another gulag-type meal, and then escorted to a large cell-like room. Standing just inside the door were two armed men wearing brown uniforms with Geheime Feldpolizei identification discs attached to them. Seated at a small table was a sergeant, who, as the guard left, directed Rosenstein to a chair at another, slightly larger table.

And then, as had been the case several days earlier, a rather small German major strutted through the door and plopped down onto the other chair. Major Manz, starting to implement the program that Brummeir had given him—on Heydrich's order, which he had developed—said in good but stilted English, "So we meet again. All right, let's begin."

Pulling some papers out of his briefcase, Manz glanced at the one on top and asked the first question. "Why did you return to France?"

"I don't know what you mean, 'return to France.'"

"Come now, Lieutenant, we have witnesses who saw you arrive on the boat that loaded the trucks and soldiers that then sailed out of Cherbourg Harbor, leaving you behind. You gave the impression that you and your men were protecting their departure. However, you didn't fire a shot, and you quickly surrendered—rather a cowardly action for a professional British soldier.

"And the act you played, the William Lessing middle-name farce. How did you know that Oberst Wilhelm—the German equivalent of William—Lessing was conducting interrogations?"

Rosenstein's mind was racing as he heard the questions. He didn't understand what Manz was talking about. He remained silent.

"Come on, Lieutenant, answer me."

"I am Lieutenant Jacob W. L. Rosenstein. As a prisoner of war, that is all I am required to tell you."

"Ah, the Rosenstein ploy. Your story about how you got the name sounded like a farce to me. What were you hoping to achieve? Come on, Lieutenant, speak up. Ah, Lieutenant. What is your real rank or title?"

"I am Lieutenant Jacob William Lessing Rosenstein. That is all I am required to tell you. And it is all I will."

For more than an hour, the act went on. Manz didn't raise his voice as he kept repeating the same and similar questions. And Rosenstein kept giving the same answer. Finally, Manz gave an order in German and the two Geheime Feldpolizei officers each grabbed an elbow and more or less dragged the prisoner back to the cell with its metal human-waste pot.

For the next five days this act was essentially repeated. For nourishment the prisoner was given two cups of water and three slices of bread and some boiled cabbage as a daily ration. On the sixth day he was awakened before dawn, led to a shower, and surprisingly, while he ate a full breakfast wearing only his undershorts, his uniform was being cleaned. Or so he thought. Feeling much better after finishing his breakfast, he was escorted not to his cell, but down to the basement, where his two escorts opened a door into a dark cell, threw him to the floor, essentially naked, and slammed the door shut.

The only light was a dim line under the door. After a few minutes, he was able to see objects in the cell. Except there were no objects. There was not even a pot for his wastes. He slumped down onto the floor by the door. The hours passed. How many, he didn't know, for his watch had been taken when he entered the shower. After a while, he began to count: one, two, three, four … Approximately a second for each number. Sixty for the first minute; 3,600 for the first hour. By the time he reached 6,000, each number was closer to two seconds long than one. Then three. Before he reached 7,000, he had fallen asleep. Hours later, he was awakened by the need to urinate. But where? He chose the corner farthest from the door. The result of the full breakfast joined the liquid hours later. Hours of misery. Even though it was summer, he was shivering from the cold. The room temperature felt like it was winter.

He had heard a slight sound somewhere in the room. He had finally located a small fan in the ceiling, near the back wall of the cell, blowing cold air across the room to the crack under the door. He curled up in the corner of the room opposite his waste area. The hours passed with periods of sleep and awakenings. During the latter, he thought about pleasant memories of his life before and during that day with Oberst Lessing. He remembered Major Manz's comment in German: "He bears somewhat of likeness." No, his comment was "resemblance to you." Was it possible?

Manz: he hadn't seemed such a bad person during the interview. Just a soldier. Why him? During the past day—or had it been two? Pretty rough—no, while very rough—no, it was really bad. Was it just a preamble to something even worse?

Manz! What was the purpose of the mistreatment he was subjecting him to? Was this normal German treatment of British prisoners? If not, why him? Although his mission was somewhat different, there was nothing too unusual about it. Saving men and equipment was always a military objective. It must be the "Lessing" thing. Just a coincidence or something more? And what next? He was thirsty and hungry and cold.

Let's have a better memory. Ah, Mary! His "cousin." Daughter of David, the brother of his adopted father, Jacob, whose home was

115

next door to his. In their preteen years they had been like brother and sister. They were not blood related, and by their late teens they were much, much more; in their early twenties they had become husband and wife. This pleasant memory soon caused him to drift into unconsciousness.

He was awakened by the sound of the dungeon door opening. His two handlers entered and escorted him—actually almost carried him—back to his cell. Inside was a large basin of hot water, his cleaned uniform, including his shoes but no watch, and, wonder of wonders, a complete meal with a large pitcher of water. And a metal pot! An hour or so later, after he had cleaned himself, donned his uniform, and satisfied his hunger, the cell door opened and Manz entered.

"Ah, Lieutenant Lessing, Rosenstein—if it is lieutenant and Lessing—how have the last two days been? You have a choice: treatment according to the Geneva standards or continuation of the past two days. Tell me, what is the Rosenstein ploy? I repeat, your story about how you got the name sounds like a farce to me. What were you hoping to achieve? Come on, Lieutenant, speak up. Ah, is it really lieutenant? What is your real rank or title?"

CHAPTER TWENTY-EIGHT

HAMBURG, GERMANY
JULY 8, 1940

After Schmidt left, Lessing called Majorgeneral Oster and received permission to come to his office. When he had been announced by his Unteroffizier and entered his office, Oster was pouring himself a cup of coffee from a pitcher, which he placed on a small table when his cup was full. After they had exchanged the appropriate military greetings, he pointed to a chair by his desk. Lessing sat down and began the recitation of what he had learned from Feldwebel Schmidt. When he had finished, Oster poured another cup of coffee, having emptied the previous one during the recitation. He motioned for Lessing to pour himself some. For the next several minutes he was silent as he in turn took sips from his cup.

The general then said, "Perhaps it's time to get ahold of Major Manz. He may be the key to finding this Rosenstein. The Englishman Bradford has indicated through Pasht's agent, Juhol, that he has prepared a lengthy summary of Britain's analysis of Sealion for delivery on an agreed date, which is the twentieth, five days from now. Franco has agreed to serve as a neutral party.

"Therefore Bradford will meet Juhol at the Spanish embassy in Lisbon on the twentieth and give him his handwritten analysis of his country's defensive plan against Sealion. Vice Admiral Buckner is sending two of his military evaluation experts there. They will review the plans to make certain that they are realistic. If they say they aren't, Rosenstein will be taken to a POW compound. After all, Bradford is from the other side, and this might just be a hoax on us. That being the case, we'll get back to our regular functions. If so, we have not spent much of our resources on it. It won't be the first time we have been hoaxed. Forget that last remark and get to work," Oster said with a slight smile.

He then continued. "However, if they say the plans are realistic, you will deliver his grandson to him at the Spanish embassy in Lisbon on the twenty-second."

Lessing of course agreed. Within two hours of returning to his office, he had made contact with Manz in Brussels. Lessing informed him that Admiral Canaris needed some information about the results of their program and that the two of them should get together as soon as possible to discuss this.

He told Lessing he was on an important assignment; could he come to Brussels for the meeting? Lessing hesitated for a few moments, thinking. Time was important; why argue? "Of course. I'll fly in tomorrow. Where are you?"

"At Stalag Saint-Gilles."

Contacting Oster's assistant, Lessing had him arrange an early-morning flight to Brussels.

As Lessing lay in bed that night, he reviewed the situation of his dual identity.

He was doing his duty as Oberst in Germany's Abwehr: a special assignment, a program they thought might possibly reveal Britain's reaction to Sealion. Actually, unbeknownst to them, that assignment was being carried out by Germans for him. Lessing marveled at Winston Churchill's generosity in using what he was sure were resources that England could ill afford to use in its war effort on a program to return his son home. On second thought, though, England would benefit. They were just paying in advance for getting the service of a secret agent high in the German military hierarchy.

What will happen when Fish Boat is finished—whether it's successful or not? he thought. Although Germany is also using its resources, which are currently many times that of Britain, they are just resources, material, and people's time. The next step he would be involved in would involve people, but not just their time. Physical injury, including death would most likely become involved. Suddenly, thoughts of German people brought a real person to his mind: Hilga! And that night so long ago, which had not been affected by his amnesia. Within the last week he had learned that in addition to his son, he had a daughter. Lessing visualized her as he dropped off to sleep.

CHAPTER TWENTY-NINE

STALAG SAINT-GILLES, BRUSSELS
JULY 9, 1940

Arriving at ten o'clock after the two-hour, 300-mile flight from Hamburg to a small airfield just outside the built-up area of Brussels, Lessing was met by a military policeman driving a black sedan. When he opened the back door, Lessing saw Manz. He apparently was skeptical about the reason for having to meet, three weeks after their presentation to the admiral. He appeared eager to find out the real reason for their contact. On the way to where his assignment was, Lessing related his made-up tale, which would actually become the ruse that had developed into the admiral's and the general's exchange program.

"The British have communicated to our embassy in Madrid through the Spanish ambassador to Britain, Gomez, and Francisco Franco. They are interested in an exchange of prisoners. Because of Franco's relationship with the admiral, they contacted him rather than the Führer. Specifically, they have captured Hermann Rigel, the captain of one of our sunken U-boats. They have said that if we agree, they want a list of our POWs who were captured in June to determine who they want in the exchange.

"The admiral is suspicious of their request. However, he wants to play along with it for a while to see where it may lead. I guess the last prisoners we were involved with in the middle of June were those in Cherbourg—the day I was hit on the head. If I recall correctly, they were captured at the harbor's dock. Their commander was that officer who had a middle name somewhat similar to mine.

"What was his last name?" Lessing asked nonchalantly. "Do you know where they are?"

"It is Rosenstein. They are at Stalag Seven A. It's in Moosburg, near Munich."

"Oh yes, Rosenstein. But Stalags are for enlisted men," Lessing replied, his German mind with its recall seemingly completely joined up with his English one. He ccontimued "Where is the prisoners' commander, Rosenstein?"

Manz hesitated, and then said, "I don't know. The last I saw of him, he was loaded on a POW train with the enlisted men of his company."

The sedan had arrived at a large three-story masonry building with wings radiating from a central round core. Manz started to open the door. Lessing reached over and grabbed his wrist, keeping the door closed.

"What are you doing?" Manz gasped. The driver started to open his door.

"You keep yours closed too," Lessing ordered. "That's an order, from an Oberst."

He did so, looking at Manz questioningly.

Manz started to speak.

"Shut up and listen," Lessing said. "Admiral Canaris has given me absolute authority on this matter. Don't lie to me, Major. I know that you and Brummeir are up to something with Rosenstein. I know that you ordered Sergeant Schmidt to deliver Rosenstein to Brummeir at the prisoner-holding facility on June 19, more than three weeks ago. Actually he may be the one the British want. Our agent Johol has found out he has relatives who are high up in the government. So tell me. Where is he?"

Lessing noticed that Manz had seemingly automatically turned his head slightly toward the building when he first asked where. This time he turned his head away from the building.

"Ah, so he's here," Lessing said. "The subject of your current assignment? What are you and Brummeir up to? Answer me! That's an order, Major. Not just from me, a superior officer, but through me, from Admiral Canaris."

Manz had flinched when Lessing said Brummeir's name. He now hesitated. However, as Lessing again started to say, "Where—," he showed his inability to defy a direct command.

"Lieutenant Colonel Brummeir is in charge. We can contact him inside."

Lessing ordered Manz to tell him the reason for the three-week attempt to get Rosenstein to admit he was a British agent; as he talked, Lessing jotted notes on a small sheet of paper.

Manz said, "Brummeir and Obergruppenführer Heydrich were concerned about Rosenstein for several reasons, including how easily he was captured, his strange middle names—in essence the same as yours—and his overall reaction to being a POW."

Lessing and Manz entered the building, going to Manz's office. There, Manz arranged a three-way telephone call with Brummeir, himself, and Lessing. And Lessing began the implementation of the general's ruse. (Actually it was a furtherization of Churchill's for Lessing.)

Lessing told Manz that the exchange of prisoners story was just a ruse to get to Rosenstein. It had worked. And that the real purpose for getting him was the possibility of getting him to become an agent for Germany.

Lessing then related General Oster's fantastic program for the development of a superspy for the Abwehr. He didn't relate the fact that the program would be an integral part of Churchill's Fish Boat. Lessing told Manz, "Amazingly, it is possible we will be able to use your treatment of Rosenstein, who for some obscure reason you think is a British agent, in the implementation of his conversion to our side, which is to make him a double agent for Germany."

After a half hour or so of discussion, Lessing's use of sugar and pepper finally got Brummeir to agree to his plan. And at Lessing's suggestion, Brummeir had done so without consulting with his superior, Heydrich, which surprised Lessing. One usually didn't trifle with Heydrich. As it turned out, it was for him a grievous mistake.

CHAPTER THIRTY

STALAG SAINT-GILLES, BRUSSELS

JULY 9, 1940

Before Lessing and Manz met with Rosenstein in his cell in the late afternoon, the two of them had an early lunch. When they finished, Lessing told Manz he needed an hour or so to prepare his plan for their meeting. When Lessing retired to the room Manz had secured for him, he wrote a short message in a code based on notes he had written down during Manz's recitation in the sedan.

When Manz and Lessing entered his cell, Rosenstein was leaning against the back wall, his head hanging down. He apparently had completed his midday exercise routine. He spent a half hour or so walking around the cell and doing pushups on the floor, once when he woke up in the morning and again in the afternoon after the final meal of the day, regardless of which cell he was in. Over the two-plus weeks, with the meager and limited variety of his food and his physical exercises, Manz figured Rosenstein had lost a few pounds, including most of his body fat.

As Rosenstein looked up, he saw a rather tall German officer, with a 180-pound, muscular body and a strong-featured, slightly elongated, blue-eyed face who had ordered Manz to stand against the cell's corridor wall. Lessing took a couple of steps into the cell, and his son took a couple of steps from the wall, remaining in the dimly lighted area of the cell.

Lessing raised his right hand as he opened his mouth to speak. He spoke in English. "Please let me finish. It will last only two or three minutes." For the next minute or so there was complete silence. He was struggling to control his emotions. He was seeing his son for the first time.

At least it was the first time knowing for sure that he was his son.

"Stop!" Lessing, his father, sharply said as his son again started to speak. "You will have an opportunity to reply when I am finished. We might say a coin has been tossed and I won the first pitch. I get to talk until all the comments are out in the open. Then you have your opportunity to advance and score points for your cause. Yes, I am the officer who was involved with your interrogation a few weeks ago. Now, where was I?"

Lessing glanced down at the paper with the coded message. He then began the fiction that Oster had created. "You have lied about your name and how your parents died. We know that you were born in England, not France, that your mother's name was Mary, not Penny, and that you spent your younger years in Germany, where you have many friends. You were forced to return to England against your will when you were a teenager and your parents were killed in an auto accident.

"You speak perfect German: you have not fired a shot at any one of us. And I think you really wish you were, as you have been in cricket matches with your perfect tossed pitches, on the winning side of the present match—this conflict."

Lessing had been speaking rapidly in perfect Oxford English, placing a slight emphasis on the words cricket, tossed, pitch, matches, two or three, and Mary. Out of the corner of his left eye, he had watched Manz as he went through the tale he had rehearsed with him and he had not seemed to notice, and he probably had no idea what the game of cricket was. When he turned his head to look at the prisoner, Lessing looked down at the paper with a slight jerk and winked with his right eye.

Lessing concluded, "We know that you are a British agent, chosen because of your German experience. We want you to become an agent for Germany. All right—you can speak."

"I want to know why you are treating me so badly. I thought that Germany treated war prisoners according to the Geneva Conventions. Those rules have not been followed in these past weeks. Also you have asked about—or, more than that, accused me of—actions that are not true, hundreds of times. And I have answered them true fully hundreds of times. Now you threaten to kill me if I don't confess to something that is not true. Please tell me what it's all about. If I accept, what will I be doing? My training is as a soldier. Not a spy. I don't want to kill people as a spy. People I know—people who are my friends.

He hesitated before continuing. "People I have played card games with, even cricket with."

Lessing hesitated before replying. Cricket! He might understand the situation!

"Your duties will be to collect information that will enable us to shorten the war. The result will be less killing. If you accept, we will train you. We will give you until tomorrow to make your decision. You will have to select one of the two choices."

As Lessing followed Manz out of the cell, he turned and, speaking over his shoulder as he passed through the doorway, said, "The next several hours shouldn't be too bad. You'll have time to make your decision. I hope it's the right one."

As Lessing grasped the door's handle, he dropped the paper with a hundred or so words on it onto the floor. Looking over his shoulder, Lessing had seen the look of astonishment on his face.

As Lessing took the door's key from one of the handlers who was standing in the corridor, and locked the door, he saw it in his mind's eye being picked up by the twenty-two-year-old Englishman who had spent three of his early teen summers in Lisbon with his grandfather, the British ambassador to Portugal.

Iam not who i appear to be i am on the other your side i hope you
got the signals showing this to be true only someone on your side

would know the mik now your grandfather that is why i wrote this in this foreign tongue know your uncle and your neighbors daughter I will help you appear to be following the suggested switch but not too willingly admit that you have lied and what I said isessentially true do not trust who walked in with me complain about what he did but say you derstand why he did it ask how it is possible to make the change what rewards will you get why me finally there is reason for our names after you reads this i and memorize it destroy it

CHAPTER THIRTY-ONE

STALAG SAINT-GILLES, BRUSSELS
JULY 9, 1940

Rosenstein took the slip of paper over to the cell's small window. Studying the message, his mind recalled his summers with his grandfather, who had encouraged him to learn the native language as he had done with his son, Jacob's father, years earlier. He was able to read the message because he saw it was composed in Portuguese.

An hour later he had deciphered it. It really wasn't difficult. The words didn't have spaces between them and being in Portuguese made it impossible to read if you didn't know the language. It took awhile for his memory to bring forth the meaning of the words, but once it did, he got the true meaning of the message. If he could believe it, he was going to be rescued in some way by this German colonel.

He was sitting on the cot slowly reading, committing its contents to memory, when the door flew open and the two handlers strode into the cell. He barely had time to tuck the paper into his shirt pocket before they grasped his arms and practically carried him to the door and out into the corridor.

Down on the first floor they opened the door into not another cell but a room that looked much different. He was astonished. It was furnished like a room in an expensive hotel. Across the room a door was open into another room, not with a pot, but with a toilet! And there was not a cot but a luxurious bed, upon which lay the spotless uniform of a British lieutenant.

Standing by the bed was a sergeant who addressed him in English. "Welcome, Lieutenant Rosenstein. The Oberst requests that you stay in this room while you consider what he has offered. He will come here tomorrow to consult with you. I suggest you take the necessary steps to get into your new uniform." He pointed to the open door of the bathroom and then the uniform.

He gestured to the handlers to leave the room, and as he followed them, he said, "Your dinner will be brought here in about an hour."

Rosenstein was baffled by the miraculous change of events. He collapsed into the well-cushioned chair in front of a nice-looking table. Then the truth hit him. Of course, they were trying to influence his decision. Well, why not take advantage, get cleaned up, eat what was probably going to be a good meal, and then try to relax and consider his alternatives?

He started with an extended shower, during which he brushed up on his German. It had been two years since he had left Cambridge, where he (and, he had been told, his father) had majored in the German language. Finally stepping out of the shower, he shaved off three weeks of whiskers with the razor that was available, walked over to the bed, and put on the uniform, which fit perfectly. A pair of well-shined black boots stood on the floor beside the bed. He put them on. Seeing his reflection in the mirror on the wall, clean, shaved, hair combed, he suddenly felt good. So much so that he did a little dance, swinging his new boots in the air. After eating the delivered good meal, he mentally reviewed what his action would be the next day. He looked at his watch, which he had found on the room's table. It was almost midnight. He took off his new uniform. Lying down on the luxurious bed, he was asleep within minutes.

CHAPTER THIRTY-TWO

STALAG SAINT-GILLES, BRUSSELS
JULY 10–11, 1940

He was awakened by a knock on the door. He looked at his watch: almost six o'clock. In German he asked, "What do you want?"

"The Oberst wants you in an hour. I have your breakfast."

"Give me a couple of minutes."

He quickly got up and put on the new uniform. As he bent over to put on the boots and saw the dirty old uniform on the floor beside them, he picked it up to put it into the room's waste container. But first he reached into the shirt pocket for the message paper. It wasn't there!

He frantically searched through the uniform's other pockets. Nothing. He searched around the room, under the bed, under the chair cushions, across every inch of the floor. Nothing! He tried to recall everything that had happened since he had put it in his pocket. There was nothing relating specifically to the paper. It had just dropped out of sight.

The room's door opened and the sergeant came in, leaving a third person who was holding a tray with food on it, in the passageway. Noticing the harried look on Rosenstein's face, he asked in English, "Is something wrong?"

Not wanting to reveal the presence of the note, Rosenstein forced himself to calm down as he replied, "No."

"Come on, you're not eating here. I'm Sergeant Hecker," he said as he took Rosenstein's left elbow. As he almost dragged him out of the room, Rosenstein's left foot was pulled across the room's fancy carpet, thereby scraping off the piece of paper that was stuck to the boot's sole.

As he ate his breakfast, his mind was whirling. How serious was the loss of the paper? Probably no problem. Just another scrap of paper destined for the trash. He turned his mind to the problem of who he was to be.

While he was considering the paper's plight, three prisoners, one of the Stalag's cleaning battalion crews, were entering the vacated room. As the handler stood guard in the doorway, they quickly cleaned the room. As they left, one of them noticed the piece of paper near the door, picked it up, and dropped it into the wastebasket.

When the crew finished its day's work in midafternoon, they took the cleaning tools back to the supply room. The contents of the wastebasket were dumped onto the loading table leading to one of the building's furnaces.

The wastes from the scores of cells in the Stalag as well from the rest of the facility were sorted by low-paid inhabitants of Brussels, who removed usable items, such as discarded clothing that could be laundered and used as cleaning rags, as well as other useful items that by error had been collected as waste, such as pencils, pens, and salvageable metal objects.

One of the latter was the buckle on a salvageable belt, which, as it was removed from the table, scooped up a piece of paper lodged in the buckle. As the belt was tossed into the salvage bin, the paper became dislodged and fluttered down, not into the bin, but into the nearby empty metal lunch container of one of the workers. Later a worker entered the area, picked up the empty containers, and returned them to the building's massive kitchen.

The next day, Sergeant Hecker, Manz's assistant, was eating his lunch before joining his superior and Oberst Lessing in the continued interrogation of the British lieutenant.

The previous afternoon, carrying out the major's order, he had contacted Sergeant Pacher in Berlin and arranged a telephone connection with their commanding officer, Lieutenant Colonel Brummeir. After completing his call, the major had instructed him to have the managers of the prison provide a special room for the British prisoner.

This day he removed the bowl from the lunch container and ate its contents, and as he started to place the bowl back in, he saw the piece of paper on the bottom of the lunch container. Curious, he picked it up. He couldn't understand the scribbling in a language he couldn't read. Glancing at his watch, he pushed the paper aside, hastily stood up, and left the room. The next day as he gathered his material for his return with Major Manz to their SS headquarters in Berlin, the piece of paper was accidentally included with other papers in his pouch.

CHAPTER THIRTY-THREE

STALAG SAINT-GILLES, BRUSSELS
JULY 10, 1940

The previous afternoon, after the session with his son, Lieutenant Jacob W. L. Rosenstein, Lessing had called the majorgeneral and reported the status of his plan. Major Manz surprisingly had seemed to accept the situation. He had suggested that the lieutenant be given a special room while he considered his choices, and he had arranged it. He had also arranged for the meeting with Rosenstein to take place not in his overnight quarters, but in the same room he had used for his previous interrogations with the British prisoner. However, he would be served a very good breakfast, thus reminding him of the two options, one of which he had to choose.

The major's reasoning was that with the room reminding him of the discomfort of the past weeks, he might be more inclined to accept the alternative.

As the two of them had dinner, they had discussed the next day's proceedings. Lessing had agreed with his reasoning of the room selection. And he had Manz relate in detail the actions of the previous weeks. After dinner, they went to the interrogation room, where they discussed the plan for the next day, July 10. At nine, Lessing had had enough for the day and retired to the room Manz had secured for him. Before he retired, he jotted down on a slip of paper, again in Portuguese, a condensed version of the notes he had made on the ride to the Stalag, followed by "Remember the message."

Lessing was wakened at dawn by the sound of heavy summer rainfall. Looking at his watch, he noted that it was about time for one of the most memorable days of his dual life to begin. After taking a quick shower, he noticed that his uniform was gone. Then, remembering Manz's suggestion as they parted the night before, he opened the room's door and picked up his uniform and shoes, which had been cleaned and polished while he slept.

Manz was already in the officers' dining hall when Lessing entered. As he sat down across the dining table from him, Manz told him that Rosenstein was already in the room. At six, Lessing assumed the schedule that he had devised had begun. Manz said Rosenstein had been awakened by Sergeant Hecker and taken to the interrogation room. They had seated him in one of the four chairs in the room. It faced the other three. After giving him a pitcher of water and a cup to drink with the breakfast that was on the tray, they had left, locking the door behind them.

Finishing a leisurely breakfast and noting that the ten o'clock time for the day's events to really begin was several hours away and that the summer rain shower had stopped, Lessing nodded at Manz and went outside. He whiled away the next few hours walking around the center streets of Brussels. At ten o'clock, Manz, Schmidt, and Lessing entered the room and sat in the three chairs. He had included Schmidt because he had obviously become a major player in the Abwehr's ruse.

Their prisoner had been slumped down, the empty breakfast tray on the floor beside his chair. He quickly sat up when they entered. For the next minute or so, there was complete silence as the three stared at him and he at them.

Then Lessing spoke, in English. "Good morning, Lieutenant. Although it probably hasn't been a too pleasant a morning for you. As breakfast was several hours ago, you are hungry, I'm sure. The sooner we finish our business, the sooner you will eat. For now we will talk in English.

"As I said yesterday, we know that you are a British agent. We want you to become an agent for Germany." Lessing paused as the prisoner started to speak.

"Go ahead—speak."

"I'm really confused," Rosenstein said. "After yesterday's session until this morning, you were treating me like a favorite of Hitler."

"When you speak of the Führer, you always say 'the Führer,' never just his last name," Manz interjected angrily.

"All right, the Führer. Let me finish. Last night a splendid room, a wonderful meal, a comfortable chair to read in—that is if I had had anything to read—and a comfortable bed, but then this morning, like a damn prisoner again."

His comment about the chair had been made with a slight rise in his voice as he looked directly at Lessing. He noted that Manz had reacted to this with a quizzical look on his face.

Lessing quickly said, "The treatment has been just to remind you that there are two different ways of your future life for you to choose from. One, to serve the people you seemingly love and respect. The other, the life of a prisoner." He paused. "Or maybe no life at all. The choice is up to you. And it must be made today, as we," he said, looking first at Manz and then at Schmidt, "have other things of importance to do."

Rosenstein's next comment was blurted out in a loud voice that was almost a scream.

"Why are you doing this? What do you think I can do for Germany if I accept your offer? How could I get away with being a spy? I'm just a common lieutenant who happens to speak German, as well as some other languages such as Portuguese. I don't have any connections with British war officials or ranking officers." He lowered his voce as he said, "What kind of life will I have?"

Lessing nodded at Manz, who replied in German. "Oberst Lessing will take control of you. Incidentally he probably is a blood relative of yours. One of his grandfathers quite likely was one of your great-grandfathers. You will become an agent for the Abwehr. He will take you to Hamburg for the training you will need to do your undercover work. I can't see why you won't accept our offer."

He continued. "But then, of course you probably are already an agent. For the enemy. However, if you are, you're a good one, as the past weeks haven't broken you. And of course, if you are a British agent, we're sure you will accept our offer: what better way to spy against a country than to have them think you are their agent? And the fortitude you have shown with your steadfastness will stand for you if you accept. However, if you accept our offer and, as we believe, are quite possibly an agent for the enemy, this means you will be a double agent. We will find this out, and if you are not ours, our treatment these past weeks will seem like a vacation, compared to what will—"

Lessing broke in. "That's enough, Major," he said in German. Continuing in English, he said, "Well, I think we have told enough for the lieutenant to make his decision." Looking at his watch, he continued, "We will be back at one." He nodded at Rosenstein, his son.

The three rose and left the room. As Lessing passed through the doorway, he reached down and took the tray of food that Sergeant Hecker, who was sitting in the hallway, was holding. Turning around, his body filling the doorway, he held out the tray toward the lieutenant. He rose from the chair and took the tray, including the slip of paper that had slipped out of Lessing's uniform sleeve and under the plate on the tray. He then turned, passed through the doorway, closing the door behind him.

CHAPTER THIRTY-FOUR

BRUSSELS TO HAMBURG

JULY 11, 1940

Being sure what the result would be, the amazing, ever-efficient Manz had arranged for the three-hour return to Hamburg by air that afternoon for Lessing, Schmidt, and the new Hauptman Lessing. As he and Sergeant Hecker were flying to Berlin, the five of them, in the late afternoon, rode together in the automobile taking them to the airfield. On the way Lessing complimented Manz on his assistance.

He of course had been right in his assumption that they would succeed. And he didn't know about the one hundred similar words that were on the slip of paper. When Schmidt had opened the door at one o'clock and the three of them again entered, the former war prisoner had stood up from the chair, saying in German as he raised his right hand in a military salute, "Hauptman Rosenstein, reporting for duty."

Again Lessing was amazed by Manz. Almost immediately his assistant, Sergeant Hecker, appeared with a German lieutenant's uniform for the new German agent. And it fit!

As had been the case with the British Auro two-engine airplane, the plane had accommodations for four passengers and two pilots. Lessing had Schmidt join the lone pilot in the cockpit while he and his son were alone in the passenger area. The son didn't know that they were father and son, only that they might be distantly related. With the roar of the engine assuring privacy, Lessing revealed, to his seemingly forced amazement, that he was in effect a double agent for Britain. He didn't relate his double identity situation.

Before he could continue, Jacob interrupted him.

"I deciphered your messages. It seems to be working out. What's next?"

Lessing then explained that the German plan of making him an agent for Germany that he and Manz had related to him was, unknown by Manz, in reality an Abwehr exchange plan of a released prisoner (him) for the British defense reaction to Germany's Sealion invasion, which, although having essentially the same result, at least for Britain, was actually a British plan of his two grandfathers, called Fish Boat, for their grandson's release from captivity.

The Abwehr plan was to keep him for a few days at the headquarters in Hamburg, appearing to advise him on the role of being an agent. Then, on the nineteenth, they would start moving him to Madrid. The final leg would be to Lisbon on the twenty-second to meet Bradford for the exchange. As Lessing had arranged the exchange, he would escort him to Madrid. From there, they would meet Pasht' agent Juhol, who would go with them to Lisbon, where the exchange would take place.

But problems would develop.

CHAPTER THIRTY-FIVE

BERLIN, GERMANY
JULY 11–14, 1940

Manz and Hecker arrived in Berlin late in the evening. Before Manz retired for the night, he directed the Feldwebel to compile the notes and summation of the interrogation of the Rosenstein project for their meeting with their superior, Oberstleutenant Brummeir, to discuss the Rosenstein/Lessing situation, which was scheduled for the next morning. After breakfast, the major arrived at Hecker's desk just as he was assembling all the notes he had taken during the previous weeks. As he did so, a piece of paper, half the size of all the others, fluttered to the floor.

"What's that?" Manz asked.

"Oh, it's just a piece of wastepaper that I found in one of the lunch containers. I looked at it, but it's just a lot of gibberish. It must have gotten something sticky from the lunch container on it and stuck to one of the sheets."

He bent over and picked it up and started to put it his wastebasket.

"Wait," Manz said as he reached out and took it from Hecker's hand. "Let me see it."

Holding it in his left hand he looked at it for a couple of minutes. The sergeant glanced at his watch and said, "It's time, sir."

"Right. Here," Manz said, handing the page back to Hecker. "When we're through with our meeting, take this to the foreign-reports people and see if they can figure it out."

When Manz arrived at his desk the morning of the 12th, he found the message page attached to a larger sheet with the following typed on it, the Portuguese having been translated into German.

I am not who I appear to be I am on the other your side I hope you got the signals showing this to be true only someone on your side would know them I know your grandfather that is why I wrote this in this foreign tongue I know your uncle and your neighbor's daughter I will help you appear to be following the suggested switch but not too willingly admit that you have lied and what I said is essentially true do not trust who walked in with me complain about what he did but say you understand why he did it ask how it is possible to make the change what rewards will you get why me finally there is reason for our names after you read this and memorize it destroy it.

Sitting at his deck Manz mulled over what the words might mean. He called the Stalag in Brussels to trace the path of the piece of paper. Manz was not stupid. By noon, after hearing from the administrative head of the Stalag, he had pieced together a possibility. There was the possibility that the paper had, through chance, come from Rosenstein's cell. He remembered Oberst Lessing's comments to Rosenstein: "only ones—signals—coin flip—cricket—teams—score points—not who I appear to be—other side—know grandfather—reason for names." And Rosenstein's "chair" and "to read" comments.

Names: Oberst Lessing; Jacob William Lessing. Of course. He pieced together a possible scenario from what he knew.

1. Oberst Lessing's sudden interest when he heard Rosenstein's voice during the Cherbourg interrogation.

2. Obergruppenführer's order to conduct the repeated daily questioning of Rosenstein when he heard about the Lessing/Lessing name coincidence.
3. Did this mean that Oberst Lessing was not who he appeared to be? Was the amnesia problem just a ruse of some sort?
4. Should he contact Admiral Canaris? No, remembering Heydrich's "traitor Canaris" comment. Should he ask the SS section for help? Yes, but first he should take his suspicions to his superior, Oberstleutnant Brummeir. Or should he? If he did, Brummeir would quite possibly have a problem approving an intelligence operation request that was made without reporting to his superior Heydrich, the number-two man in the SS, who hated Canaris. And the fact that Brummeir had worked with an Oberst in Canaris's Abwehr, especially one Heydrich had expressed some concern about, without consulting him.

However, time was critical. Three days had passed since the new Abwehr agent had been created. He had to do something. A new thought occurred to him: why not bypass Brummeir and make the request directly to Heydrich, who for sure would become aware of what was happening? That would probably be the end of Brummeir. There would then be a vacancy, the need for someone to become the head of the SS subunit.

And who would be the obvious choice? Major Adolph Manz. Or make that Lieutenant Colonel Adolph Manz! But wait, tell Heydrich only about the creation of the spy, not about his suspicion of a secret Abwehr plot. He would investigate and act on his own. That way if he was wrong, the SS chief wouldn't know.

CHAPTER THIRTY-SIX

GERMANY
JULY 11-16, 1940

When the two Lessings arrived in Hamburg, even though it was around nine in the evening, there was a sedan, with Julian, waiting for them, welcoming the Oberst and the new lieutenant. Which meant, Lessing thought, that Julian realized that two Lessing names was just a coincidence with no personal relationship.

They were at the admiral's office, facing him and General Oster before ten. Canaris was most pleased with the success of Oster's ruse. He would score high with Hitler when the Sealion invasion would succeed because the Abwehr had delivered details of the enemy's defensive plan.

Lessing felt a touch of sorrow, because the plan that he would deliver to Canaris would, although appearing accurate, not be even close to being authentic. He liked the admiral, even after finding that his dual identity meant that he became part of the enemy. But war is war. As they drank the champagne supplied by the admiral to herald the ruse's success, the conclusion was planned.

1. The next few days would be spent with people from Oberst Piekinbrock's Secret Intelligence Section, who would force-feed Hauptman, temporarily named Bach, the rudiments of being an

agent. Although the admiral, Oster, Julian, and Lessing knew he was not to be an agent, the illusion had to be continued to get him back to England. Actually, his daytime hours were spent reading some English magazines that the Abwehr had.

And during the days, the Abwehr experts made the necessary documents that might be needed. These would identify him as an Abwehr Hauptman.

He would be traveling with his superior officer Oberst Lessing. A second set of papers, to be hidden in his specially designed shoe, identified him as British. They would travel by train and bus to Basel, Switzerland, in lieu of flying, because the journey would be less conspicuous. In Basel, he would become a British citizen. Then by commercial air they would fly from Basel to Lisbon.

2. After spending the night at the Abwehr office in Lisbon, they would meet the German agent Juhol and James Bradford at the Spanish embassy. The latter had already delivered the British defense preparation plan to Germany's Sealion invasion. Lessing knew it had been reviewed by the Abwehr's two experts as being plausible. Jacob's release would consummate the Abwehr's part of the exchange.

During the days Lessing spent time, having gotten the admiral's permission, continuing to investigate the feasibility of one agent handler operation for the Abwehr. Until the late afternoon of the 15th, there was no contact between the Abwehr's new agent and the Oberst. At four o'clock, they got together in the father's quarters to finalize the plan for his return to Britain. Having done so, after the evening meal the two of them took a walk on the streets of Hamburg adjacent to the Abwehr headquarters.

Making sure they were sufficiently isolated for anyone to overhear other conversation, the father briefly related a condensed version of who he really was. "Jacob, I am more than a British agent," he said. "Until a few weeks ago, I thought—really thought—I was a German soldier. On the night after Manz and I interrogated you, a German plane accidentally dropped a bomb on the inn. It didn't explode, but a roof beam dropped down and made a glancing blow on my head. I was unconscious for a couple of days. When I woke up, I began to realize that I was not Oberst Lessing of the German army, but Lieutenant William Lessing of the British army. And also that I was your father."

On hearing the last sentence, the younger man started to slump toward the ground. His father grabbed hold of him and held him erect. For several minutes, they remained clasped in each other's arms while he broke down and cried, and for a minute or so, father joined son.

Sitting on a bench in a deserted park for the next half hour or so, Lessing related the unbelievable tale to him. When he finished, they returned to his quarters and retired, Jacob sleeping on a couch.

CHAPTER THIRTY-SEVEN

HAMBURG

JULY 15, 1940

Sergeant Hecker waited until the two had left the park before he shook the stiffness out of his legs and left the spot behind a large tree trunk, about fifty feet from the bench. He continued following them, which he had started when the two left the dining hall. When they entered the building, he figured he had completed the task and entered his sedan, which he had parked across the street from the hall, and drove to the SS's Hamburg headquarters, where he contacted his superior Lieutenant Colonel Manz, who was dozing on a couch in one of the building's offices.

"I couldn't hear what they were saying, but suddenly the younger sort of collapsed and the Oberst grabbed him and held him up. They stayed clasped together for several minutes. And it looked like the younger was crying. They then sat on a bench for about half an hour. When they left the park, they passed by close enough so that I heard some of their conversation. They were not speaking in German but in English. The few words I heard were crack of dawn, twenty-one, pack, and parts of words such as ton—, frieb—. That's all I heard."

"You be in position to follow them before any crack of dawn," Manz said. "Here, this should cover your expenses." He handed

Hecker some bills. "I'll be flying back to Berlin tomorrow morning to report to Obergruppen Heydrich. From what you heard, they could quite possibly be going to Freiburg. I'll contact our station there and have them give you any assistance you need. You know how to keep in touch with me. Every night at twenty-two hundred."

They both retired to their temporary quarters.

When Manz, back at his office in Berlin, had related the Abwehr spy plan to Heydrich on the telephone at nine o'clock in the morning, he was ordered to come to his office on Prinz Albrechtstraße at two o'clock.

When Manz arrived, he was directed to a small conference room. Heydrich was not there. However, Brummeir's assistant, Pacher, was, with a man in civilian clothes whom Pacher introduced as Himmler's SS Investigator Hoff.

"Where is the Obergruppen Heydrich?" Manz asked.

"He had other business to attend to," Pacher said. "He told me that you are in charge of the investigation, Lieutenant Colonel Manz. Yes, I said Lieutenant Colonel. Apparently Brummeir has resigned and the Obergruppen has appointed you to take charge of the unit. He said Herr Hoff can help you investigate Canaris's spy operation to see if there is more than we now know."

Shaking Manz's offered hand, Herr Hoff related what he had already found out about Oberst Lessing.

"We have a contact at Abwehr headquarters, and she got me a copy of Lessing's file. Seems he was a hero in the last conflict. A month or so before the end, he suffered a severe head wound that apparently caused him to develop what is called autobiographical amnesia. It's a very peculiar illness. Although he can remember nonpersonal things, such as foreign languages and mathematics, he can't remember a single thing about his personal life before he was wounded." Hoff paused, then continued.

"Or can he? You of course know about his getting hit in the head a few weeks ago. There are twenty-two years between two similar head wounds. During those years, he has been a gymnasium teacher and a weapons salesman as well as an officer. He is around forty to forty-five, I'd say. However, his mind seems only twenty-two. We must find out what's in the rest of his mind. With your permission, I will head south where there are people I will interview, including a Hans Brachman, who was Lessing's doctor after the accident in Cherbourg."

"You have it," Manz said. There was silence for more than a minute as he paused before speaking again. "I will go with you. I will be staying at our headquarters in Freiburg. It was damaged in last month's bombing, but it has been sufficiently restored." Turning to Pacher, he said, "Haupt-Feldwebel Pacher, you will be in charge of the unit here in Berlin while I am gone. Keep an eye on the group. Call me at Freiburg at least once first thing each morning."

"Yes, sir," Pacher replied, adding, "I understand that Private Brummeir is now a member of the Wehrmacht."

When Manz and Hoff left the room, Pacher returned to his office and, using the code that Julian had given him, reported to Julian what had occurred.

CHAPTER THIRTY-EIGHT

SCHWARZWALD (BLACK FOREST), GERMANY
JULY 15–16, 1940

Doctor Hans Brachman was finishing his post-operation cleaning process when Hilga's daughter Wilhelmnina entered the cleaning room. "There is a telephone call for you, from Obergruppenführer Heydrich—not him, actually, but a representative. Says it's very important."

"This is Doctor Brachman. Who are you? What do you want?"

"My name is Hoff. I'm calling for the Oberstgruppen. He wants some information about one of your patients, Wilhelm Lessing."

"I don't give out information about patients."

"Doctor, you are a member of the German army. You will obey orders from your superior officer. I will be there at twelve noon tomorrow, with a written order from the Obergruppenführer. Please have the information for me. Good-bye."

Hans was bewildered. Why would Heydrich's SS want information about Wilhelm? He sought out Hilga and told her about the call. For the next hour or so, they reviewed their experience with him from the weeks in 1918 and 1919 when they worked with him on his amnesia problem. They couldn't recall a thing that had happened during those weeks that the SS could be interested in. They did explore the night of conception, but did not see any reason why the SS would be interested.

When they moved ahead over twenty years to June 1940, they realized that things were not as easily dismissed. Hilga remembered his confusion about the date. At the time, she hadn't given it a second thought. Now it gave them pause.

Brachman now remembered that after Lessing first regained consciousness, he had seemed to pass into and out of unconsciousness as he and Hilga had talked to and about him. So what? Now they had to consider, was he really unconscious, or was he pretending so he could listen to what the two of them were saying to each other? But why would he do so? And the breakfast on the day he flew back to Hamburg: his mind, at the farewell breakfast, Hans now recalled, had seemed to be far away from the commandeered French hospital. And his being at the hospital: accidental or not? Putting his and Hilga's remembrances together, did that mean that perhaps Wilhelm Lessing wasn't really Wilhelm Lessing? Nonsense, of course he was.

Hilga's voice broke him out of his reverie. "I think we are making too much out of what was happening. After all, he was just beginning to recover from a bad knock on his head. Let's move ahead to a couple of weeks ago. Nothing suspicious there, other than his figuring out that Wilhelmnina was his daughter."

"I agree," Hans said. "Let's just put down on paper the bare facts in a way that shows that our relationship was purely professional. And no mention about the father/daughter relationship. After all, only the two of us and they know about it."

They spent the rest of the day, when they weren't doctoring and nursing, preparing a draft of a report. Hans dictated it to Wilhelmnina, who in addition to being a good nurse was a good typist. It was a two-page analysis of the medical treatments given to Lessing. Arising early, they reviewed it and after explaining the situation to Wilhelmnina, had her type up a final report, which they handed to Herr Hoff when he arrived at noon.

1. Their first encounter with Wilhelm Lessing was in late October 1918. He had two head wounds. One was just a crease below his nose that healed rather quickly, as did the other, which gave him a concussion. Apparently a shell had glanced off his helmet and knocked him unconscious. When he regained consciousness, he could not remember his past—that is, his personal past. He was very well educated and he could remember what he had learned, except for that which affected his personal life. He could not remember anything about his personal past, not even his name. The report then related their contact with him until he left the hospital with Fuerst in February 1919, except for the one night.

2. They were surprised to be treating him again in June 1940, not as the result of a military wound this time, but an accident. He had been hit in the head in essentially the same place as twenty-two years earlier. This time he was unconscious for only several hours, not two days, as was the case in 1918.

3. The surprise reunion a couple of weeks ago. Nothing unusual, other than the amazing coincidence of meeting again for the third time.

4. Doctor Hans Brachman's complete report of the medical treatments for each of the three occurrences.

When Hoff arrived, they invited him to join them for lunch. In between bites he perused the reports. When he finished, he said, "Thank you. Very complete. However, I have a question. The event of three weeks ago: is it possible that this was a planned 'coincidence'? If so, why?"

Brachman replied, "I don't see how it could have been. A plane crash? They all could have been killed, except for the pilot's skill. And even if it was, for what purpose?"

Hoff jotted down something in a small notebook. He then wrote on the last sheet of their report the following: "Do you both swear, on the penalty of death, that these words are the complete and true full history of your association with Wilhelm Lessing?"

He then repeated the words verbally. On hearing the word death, they stiffened and then nodded and replied in the affirmative. "Please sign," Hoff said, handing Brachman his pen. They did. He rose from the table, thanked them, and handed Brachman a card. "If you think of anything more, call me. That is my Freiburg number."

Hoff's day was not finished. As he left the hospital, his driver pulled up in a black sedan. As Hoff got in beside him, he said, "All right, to Basel as planned."

CHAPTER THIRTY-NINE

SCHWARZWALD (BLACK FOREST), GERMANY

JULY 17–18, 1940

Hans and Hilga each gave a sigh of relief. After completing the day's medical activities, they retired to Hans's suite with Wilhemnina and finished the day with glasses of champagne. That is, they almost finished the day.

As Wilhemnina was drinking her champagne, she reached into her uniform's pocket, pulled something out, and handed it to her mother.

"Look, Mother, I polished Father's medal."

"What is that? Let me see it," Hans said as he took the object out of Hilga's hand. Hilga blushed as she answered Hans's question.

"It's Wilhemnina father's, Wilhelm's, medal. The Knights Cross. I gave it to Wilhemnina a couple of weeks ago."

"Where, how did you get it?"

"On the night, er, you know ..."

Hans nodded as he looked at the bright, shiny cross. Looking at the back, he gave a startled gasp. "I thought you said it was Wilhelm's."

"It is."

"Why does it have 'Karl Josef Brachman' etched on the back?" She snatched the medal from his hand and examined its back.

"I don't understand. Wait ... Wilhemnina polishing must have erased Wilhelm's name." She gasped and sank to the floor. "Oh my God. Maybe Wilhelm is not who he says he is."

Brachman reached down and again took the medal from her hand, and looked at the name on its back.

"Karl Brachman! That's my cousin. He was listed as missing in action. How did Lessing get Karl's Knights Cross? His name on top of Karl's. His name a forgery. A spy?"

"But that was twenty years ago," Hilga said. "I don't understand."

CHAPTER FORTY

BASEL, SWTZERLAND
JULY 21, 1940

Heinrich Fuerst was sitting in the lounge of the Hotel Helvetia in Basel when Hoff came through the doorway at five o'clock. He suggested to Hoff that they have an early dinner where they could discuss whatever there was to discuss. Sixty-nine-year-old Fuerst was a Swiss citizen, not a German. Therefore, Herr Hoff had no legal authority over him as he had had over Brachman. In addition, he was a major supplier of armaments to Hitler's armies, so Hoff had to be careful about how he handled his interrogation.

"That's a good suggestion. I'm hungry. Could you also have someone serve my driver?"

"Of course." Fuerst spoke a few words to the head waiter as they entered the hotel's dining room.

After they were seated at a table in the sparsely occupied hotel dining room and each had been served a cup of coffee, Fuerst asked, "What's this about? Why is the SS interested in Oberst Lessing?"

"I don't know. But when Obergruppenführer Heydrich says do this or that, I don't hesitate. I do this or that. I know you don't have to answer. But I'm sure that you are on our side in this conflict. It is quite possible that getting this information is most important for our war effort. Therefore, I would like you to tell us all you know about Wilhelm Lessing."

"All right." For the next hour as the various dinner courses were put on the table and eaten, he related his relationship with Wilhelm Lessing. Hoff, between bites, took notes. As he listened, he noted that this Swiss industrial tycoon obviously had a deep respect for Lessing. When they had finished, Fuerst suggested that Hoff spend the night at the Helvetia.

Hoff thanked him, but declined. Leaving the hotel, he climbed in beside his driver of the black sedan and said, "All right, it's back to Freiburg, where I can send the information I've obtained today to the Obergruppenführer."

CHAPTER FORTY-ONE

SCHWARZWALD (BLACK FOREST), GERMANY
JULY 19, 1940

Hans Brachman was most disturbed. After the two women left, he spent a restless night mulling over his dilemma. He liked Wilhelm Lessing. He had even grown fond of him during those few months so long ago. But that was long ago, and these last encounters after a lifetime of no contact were, what? Only two, three days. And only medical contact, except for Wilhelmnina.

The fact that Obergruppenführer Heydrich, the number-two man in the SS, and quite possibly the number-three in the whole country, seemed to be personally involved, probably meant that its solution, whatever that was, might be most important for his country. Although he personally hated Heydrich and yes, Hitler, too, it was his country, which was at war with—was it possible?—the man called Wilhelm Lessing, who had a Knights Cross medal with his name forged over that of his "missing in action," probably dead, cousin Karl. But that was more than twenty years ago. And this man called Lessing had never mentioned its disappearance. Maybe he gave it to Hilga. That was it! It had served its purpose, naming him Wilhelm Lessing. Therefore it was not needed anymore. It had served its purpose. The placement of a spy, for future use. Why not give it, as payment, to his night's pleasure companion? Was the autobiographical amnesia just a ploy? Maybe it was and he had spent the last two decades spying for England. And he had just come back to Germany from England. If so, he was an excellent actor. Admiral Canaris evidently trusted him. He hadn't talked about where he had been. However, with Julian Fuerst's emotional, concerned chatter about his Oberst after the airplane crash, he might be able to put two and two together for four.

Finally, as the sun was rising on one of the year's longest days, he collapsed on his bed, falling into a nightmarish sleep. However, waking up a short time after dawn, he made a telephone call.

CHAPTER FORTY-TWO

VARIOUS LOCATIONS IN GERMANY

JULY 18, 1940

Leaving Hamburg, Jacob and Lessing, son and father, caught the first civilian train to Frankfort.

They were wearing civilian clothes and had Abwehr-prepared documents as railroad inspectors. In their carry-on bags were their uniforms, including side arms. Also on the train was Feldwebel Hecker, keeping discreetly out of their sight.

Five hours later, they disembarked in Frankfurt and disappeared as civilians into the Bahnhoff toilet. Reemerging, wearing the uniforms that had been in their bags as a German Oberst and his Hauptman orderly, they boarded the noon train to Freiburg. After several stops to allow military trains the right of way, they arrived in Freiburg in the late afternoon. At the Bahnhoff a call to the local Abwehr office resulted in a black sedan driving them to the Abwehr office, where a coded radio message from Majorgeneral Oster told them there was a change in the plan. The exchange would not take place in Lisbon. Agent Johol would be advised of the change by his handler, Pasht, at the embassy in Madrid. The Behr's local chief would advise them where to spend the night. Schmidt would personlly bring Lessing the details of the change.

Why a change? Lessing wondered. He would just have to wait for Schmidt, to get the why and where from the change order from General Oster.

The father and son decided to check into the Jura Hotel, as suggested by the Abwehr chief.

Passing the entrance of the hotel dining room, they soon found out the reason for the change. Seated at a table was Julian's father, Heinrich Fuerst, who waved them over to his table and asked them to join him for dinner.

During a long dinner, the elder Fuerst had an intriguing tale for them. For Lessing, it was an alarming one. He commenced by telling them about his meeting with an SS agent named Herr Hoff.

"After my interrogation by Hoff, I pondered why the interest in you, Wilhelm—that is, Oberst Lessing. I decided I would contact Julian. Even though the country is at war, my position as supplier of armaments enabled me to place a telephone call to Julian in Hamburg. Early this morning, after driving down from Basel, Switzerland, knowing of the friendly relationship between Julian and you, Wilhelm, I asked him, 'What's happening with Wilhelm?' His reply was that you were carrying out a secret Abwehr assignment and that that was all he could tell me. I then told him about Hoff's visit. He said he would look into it. He called me here at the hotel about"—he looked at his wrist watch—"four hours ago."

Summoning up Julian's report: with Majorgeneral Oster's approval, he had ordered Sergeant Schmidt, who apparently is an excellent investigator, to investigate. He contacted Sergeant Major Pacher in Berlin, who, with Manz temporarily somewhere else, now is acting head of his SS subunit, as Brummeir was no longer there, having been demoted. His successor, Lieutenant Colonel Adolph Manz, is investigating you."

He paused as Lessing gave an involuntary gasp and sputtered, "Me? Manz is investigating me? Why?" His mind was racing. Had the SS discovered his dual identity?

Fuerst then continued, "Before I go further, I should explain why Pacher gave Schmidt this information. Apparently he wants to be transferred from the SS to the Abwehr. Schmidt quickly told this to Julian, who contacted the general, who said yes. Apparently there is no love lost between Himmler and the admiral. Provided, however, the general said, that he revealed everything he knew about the SS's project about you, Wilhelm—that is, Oberst Lessing. And that he stayed on a day or two to get any additional information. The general said he would have Abwehr personnel standing by to get him from Berlin to Hamburg."

"Getting back to Manz," Lessing said.

Fuerst continued, "Some way or other, he got information that indicates perhaps you are not who you say you are. Wait," he said as Lessing started to speak. "Let me finish telling you the full story."

He continued as Lessing nodded. "During Manz's interrogation of you, Lieutenant Rosenstein, yes, Julian explained who you are, and he got hold of some kind of written information that questioned the loyalty of the Oberst. Wait," he said as again Lessing started to speak. "Please, let me finish. He informed Heydrich, who ordered the investigation. Yesterday an investigator named Hoff came here and asked me about your relationship with Doctor Hans Brachman.

"This was yesterday late afternoon, after he had talked to Doctor Brachman. Then about five a.m. this morning, Pacher called Julian and said that Brachman woke up Hoff, who was staying at the SS quarters here in Freiburg, and informed him that the Knights Cross medal that had been used to identify you twenty-two years ago had not been awarded to you but to his cousin. That your name had been forged over his cousin's. That some way or other your name had been polished off, revealing the true name.

"Hoff, knowing that Manz had accompanied him here, tried to get in touch with him at SS headquarters. However, at five in the morning, no one could find him. So Hoff then called the Berlin SS subunit, but again Manz wasn't in. So Pacher, at the time the highest rank in the office, took the message and, as he had promised, relayed it to Julian, who informed me."

He paused and motioned to a waiter to bring the three of them some coffee, and then stood up. As he walked away, he said, "I have to relieve myself. This will give you a few minutes to decide what you want to tell me."

Lessing's mind was in turmoil. Jacob was also silent as he, having learned of his father's dual identity problem the night before, could imagine his concern about what they had just heard.

Using his enumerating method, Lessing mentally listed his problems.

1. The Knights Cross! He hadn't even thought of it for more than twenty years. It must have dropped from around his neck when he was physically involved with Hilga that night so long ago. She must have kept it. And some way or another, it had surfaced. Of course! Wilhelmnina! Hilga must have given it to her because of her newfound father. Over the years the forged name slowly wore off. She must have tried to polish it, the brushing completing its removal.

2. The written message! The one he gave to Jacob? The one he couldn't find? Its code broken?

3. Manz? Himmler's spy? He had been completely satisfied with his cooperation in their project. However, at his interrogation of Jacob, his sudden interest in a prisoner—Manz knew that he had never done that before. And it was before they discovered the similar names. And the notebook Manz was referring to with Schmidt. When he had asked Manz what it was, he had said that it was just to help in making the final report. That had satisfied him, but now? Did this all add up to the conclusion that he might not be who he appeared to be? If so, would they wonder who and what the man called Wilhelm Lessing was? What would they, meaning Manz, Heydrich, Himmler, and even Hitler, do? Did the first two see that this might be an opportunity to strike a blow at the admiral and the Abwehr?

Whatever, what was he to do now, tonight? To satisfy Fuerst. Must decide quickly, as he was returning.

As Fuerst sat down, Lessing said, "I appreciate you telling me this, Heinrich. However, frankly I'm surprised that Julian has told you so much. Briefly, I and the so-called Lieutenant Lessing are on a complicated Abwehr mission—one that, even though he is unaware of it, Julian is part of. As to the Knights medal, I have no recollection at all where it came from, or why I was wearing it. As it had a name on it, I, as did many others, assumed it was my name. As to the name being forged, I have no knowledge whether it was or not."

Lessing stopped talking. Fuerst was silent for a couple of minutes, staring first at Lessing and then at Jacob, the acting German agent. He finally spoke—not in German, but in English.

"William Lessing, you are, I'm pretty sure, the father of this so-called agent. I first saw you when you were a young man, about the age your son there is now. I remember well what you looked like. If I had a picture of you two decades ago and held it up beside him, you would pass as twins. That is, except for the scars of your head wound. I suspect you are not a German but an Englishman, and that two decades ago, you did have amnesia.

"William, I believe you have regained at least part of your memory. However, I don't know what you are up to now. Whatever it is, you are quite possibly in trouble with the SS. Himmler and Heydrich are looking for ways to hit the Abwehr and the admiral.

"Wilhelm—or is it William?—I am fond of you. I believe that over the years, we have developed a good friendship. Because I don't believe you are really Oberst Lessing. At least not anymore. In fact, you may be one of Germany's enemies. But not mine. I am going to tell you the following:

"I am fond of the German people. Julian's mother was a German. However, I am not fond of the present German rulers. Yes, I have provided weapons of war. I realize now that that has been wrong. And I will attempt to stop doing so, if I can. However, I have to be careful because of Julian. After we part, I will return to my summer home here in the Schwarzwald to close some of my affairs here in Germany, and then I am leaving German soil for good. I—"

He stopped speaking as he looked over Lessing's shoulder toward the hall's entrance.

Lessing turned around and saw Sergeant Schmidt entering the dining hall. Looking past him, he saw Manz's assistant, Master Sergeant Hecker, come through the hotel's entrance and quickly disappear behind some curtains. Schmidt came over to their table and said, "Sir, Lieutenant Julian Fuerst has sent me to assist you and Lieutenant Lessing in completing the Abwehr mission. As you saw, Hecker is following me. And I'm sure his superior major—or, I mean, Lieutenant Colonel—Manz is getting reports from him. I have a water message for you from General Oster." He pulled out an envelope from an inner pocket and dropped it, to the astonishment of Heinrich and Jacob, into the water pitcher on the table.

"Don't be alarmed," Lessing said. "Just a protection in case it falls into the wrong hands. If you will excuse me, Heinrich? You too, Jacob."

Lessing picked up the pitcher and, followed by Schmidt, moved to a vacant table. There was silence for several minutes until he reached in and removed the message from its envelope. It read as follows:

Oberst Lessing—Urgent: I believe Heydrich's SS is going to try to abort your mission. As the recipient has completed his part, we in good faith must complete our portion. So we'll make the transfer of Jacob easier. Pasht will have Johol bring him to the Spanish embassy in Bern on the twenty-second at noon. Feldwebel Schmidt will assist you in completing your mission.

Lessing was silent for a few seconds as he contemplated their next move. He then, for the next few minutes, discussed it with Schmidt. Then they returned to the dinner table.

"Henrich," Lessing said, "there is some truth in what you say. However, we have a mission to complete. When it is completed, I will contact you in Switzerland, and together I hope we will be able to resolve the situation. Come, Jacob," he said as he reached into his pocket for money.

"No. It's taken care of," Fuerst said as he rose and held out his hand.

Lessing took it and asked him, "Can you help us check in? After our very long day we need to get some rest." After he did, Jacob and Lessing picked up their bags, which had been left in the hotel's foyer. After saying good-bye to Fuerst, Jacob and Lessing joined Schmidt, and the three headed over to the elevator and rode it up to the third floor. Stopping at their rooms, they opened the doors, turned on the lights, locked the doors, quickly headed to the rear stairway and down the stairs to the hotel's rear door, jumped into the sedan that Schmidt had parked there, and headed out of Freiburg, leaving Hecker behind the hotel's curtain.

CHAPTER FORTY-THREE

SCHWARZWALD (BLACK FOREST),
GERMANY
JULY 18, 1940

They thought they had evaded the SS's Hecker, and in fact they had. But obviously he was no fool. Before he entered the hotel, they surmised later, he had arranged for at least two SS men to cover the rear entrance. One of them was Brummeir, who had, by coincidence, after being demoted by Heydrich all the way down to private, the lowest-ranked member of the SS unit, been delegated to the Freiburg-area SS. He was one of the two who had been delegated to spend the night helping Hecker. When the two had been assigned to Hecker, the other member, Corporal Holtz, was the one who had met Hecker and received his instructions. Brummeir remained in the assigned truck as its driver; sitting in the truck, he was out of sight of Hecker, who was unaware of Brummeir's transfer to Freiburg but close enough to hear the conversation.

Holtz decided that the two should split up. He, having the higher rank and thereby being in command, chose the truck and left the motorcycle to Brummeir.

When Schmidt entered the isolated area outside the city, Holtz, realizing that escaping detection when driving a truck on isolated roads was difficult, gave up following him, leaving it to Brummeir on the motorcycle. Brummeir, with the wisely provided packaged food and water in the cycle's saddlebags, was able to follow the three men for the rest of the night and the following day into the second night, crafty and undetected. Finally, he was able to secretly follow them to their final destination. Parking the motorcycle in some trees, Brummeir settled down in the grove, where he was able to hide and keep watch.

CHAPTER FORTY-FOUR

SCHWARZWALD (BLACK FOREST), GERMANY

Where would they spend the three days and four nights before the meeting on the twenty-second in Bern? Although they had at least temporarily, they thought, evaded them, Manz's SS men probably were everywhere. They needed somewhere where they would be inconspicuous. They drove around the city for about twenty minutes. Schmidt, making many turns and finally satisfied that they weren't being followed, stopped on a residential street. He suggested that Hans Brachman could help them. Lessing was silent for a few moments, and then nodded and agreed.

Schmidt drove south until they were outside the built-up area of the city. He pulled over to the side of the two-lane road, got a flashlight and map out of his backpack, and spent a few minutes looking at the map. Saying that he would take a roundabout route to Schonau, he pulled back onto the road. It was close to midnight when, satisfied that no one was following them over the mountainous, curvy route, he pulled off the road and parked the car behind some trees. The three of them dropped off to sleep, or at least Lessing did. Schmidt and Jacob split the next six hours keeping awake.

Schmidt's satisfaction was too reassuring, because a quarter of a mile or so behind them, all the way from Freiburg, was a man on a motorcycle.

As the July sky began to lighten over the hills to the east, Schmidt, who had the second shift, woke up the other two when he opened the door. After the father and son relieved themselves behind some trees, Lessing looked at Schmidt's map. Showing it to the sergeant and pointing with his finger, he said, "I think we are here. Let's drive to Schonau. We'll park a couple of blocks from the hospital, and I'll go there and get Hans." The sun was fairly high in the sky when he reappeared, walking, accompanied not by Hans but by Hilga Regensburg, the head nurse at the hospital.

When Lessing had arrived at the hospital, she was sitting at a table in the dining hall drinking coffee. She expressed complete surprise when he appeared. Sitting down beside her, he explained their dilemma. When he asked where Hans was, she said he was at a medical meeting in Freiburg and would not be back until late in the afternoon. She suggested that they stay at her parents' farm, which was also her and Wilhelmnina's home. They walked back to the car, where Lessing explained to Jacob and Schmidt where they were going to stay. Nurse Regensburg got into the front seat and spoke some words to Schmidt. Schmidt started the car as soon as Lessing joined Jacob in the rear seat. A few minutes later, after abandoning the paved main two-lane road, for a one-lane gravel one, they pulled onto a long graveled driveway, which, after curving around a slight hill, ended at an open area in front of a large farmhouse and some auxiliary buildings.

Hilga had telephoned her parents that she was bringing home three guests for breakfast. She spoke to Wilhelmnina, saying that one of the men was her father but that because he was on a military mission, their father/daughter relationship was not to be mentioned. Standing in front of the buildings were an elderly couple, a man younger than they were, and a much younger, attractive woman.

Hilga introduced them as her father, brother Leopold, and two Wilhelmninas, her mother and her daughter.

Father Lessing had trouble controlling himself as he saw his son and daughter together for the first time. He had not told Jacob that he had a half-sister. His assignment did not include stopping between Freiburg and Bern. Therefore, if the plan had not been changed, they would not have met her. Even though they now had met, with Jacob leaving the country in a couple of days, he thought it best not to complicate his son's rescue. Jacob had enough on his mind, and such a meeting would certainly do so. As he and Hilga were coming back to the car, they had agreed that the father/daughter relationship would not be mentioned. In addition, Lessing had introduced Jacob to Hilga as an Abwehr soldier, keeping the father/son and half-brother/sister relationship a secret from the two. The introductions were completed when Hilga introduced her parents, Max and Wilhelmnina, and her brother Leopold to Oberst Lessing and Lieutenant Bach. Lessing waved toward Schmidt, who was standing by the car. "This is Sergeant Schmidt, who is making sure our mission is completed." Turning to Max, Lessing asked, "Where can he hide the auto?" With the vehicle hidden away in the barn, and with Leopold remaining outside, the rest of them went inside, where the three had their first meal of the day. For most of the rest of the long daylight hours of the summer day, the three of them stayed inside. Hilga and Wilhelmnina returned to the hospital in their parents' car while the other three went about doing their regular farm work, keeping watch for outsiders. An hour before darkness descended, Leopold showed the three Abwehr men around the area to help them serve as sentinels when it was their turns. With this showing and the semi-light of a full moon, they were able to move around the area rather freely. Lessing took the first three hours, Schmidt's turn was the three hours after midnight, and Jacob's were the final hours until the dawn of July 20.

Schmidt didn't try to get some sleep before his turn. When Wilhelmnina returned home in the late afternoon, she was met at the front door by twenty-six-year-old Karl Schmidt. Before his shift started, a few minutes before midnight, the two of them spent several hours learning about each other. Relieving Schmidt, Jacob was walking by the back of the building where the car was parked, when he saw movement through some trees. Removing his pistol from its holster, he walked toward the trees. As he entered the woods, there was movement behind him. His next coherent recollection was halfway through the next day, July 21.

CHAPTER FORTY-FIVE

SCHWARZWALD (BLACK FOREST), GERMANY
JUNE 20–21, 1940

On Saturday, July 20, Hilga woke up Dr. Hans Brachman by calling his personal telephone just before dawn. Stretching the truth, she said that there was a seriously injured soldier whose vehicle had run off the road and hit a tree.

Hans said she should bring him to the hospital. She replied that he was trapped in the vehicle and they could not get him out. He needed immediate aid before he could be moved. And she couldn't do it.

"Where is he?" he asked.

"Pick me up here at the farm and I'll show you."

He arrived about twenty minutes later, driving his Mercedes convertible sedan up to the front door, where Hilga was standing in the open doorway. He quickly got out of his car as she stepped forward, grasped his arm, and pleaded, "Please come in. It is dangerous to stay outside. Sergeant Schmidt will put your car in the barn."

As she said that, Schmidt stepped by her and got into the black sedan. As he drove it into the barn, the barn door was opened by Leopold.

Hans's body stiffened and he started to sputter. "What's going—"

Lessing stepped through the doorway and grasping his other arm said, "Please, Hans, come in. The lieutenant needs your help. We must close the door. I'll explain what's going on."

He led the shocked Hans, the doctor, into the room where Jacob lay on a bed. The upper portion of his head was covered by a bandage, and his left arm was wrapped tightly against his chest.

Upon seeing Jacob, Dr. Brachman stepped forward, and for the next half hour or so, there was silence as the doctor practiced his profession. Finally, standing up he said, "I don't think it's too serious. I've stitched up the gash in his chest. It isn't deep enough to be serious. The arm is badly bruised, and some ribs are probably cracked. As to the head, there is concussion. How serious, we will have to wait until he wakes up to find out. He should be taken to the hospital. Now, Wilhelm Lessing—if indeed it is Wilhelm Lessing—what's going on here?" He stood up, walked over to where the Oberst and the nurse were sitting, stood in front of them, and stared down at them.

Lessing replied, "First, the current situation. Jacob—yes, my son—and I are on a mission for Admiral Canaris's Abwehr. You probably are unaware that Himmler's SS wants to get rid of the admiral and take over the Abwehr. And for some reason they—that is, my aide on a former project, Major Manz—seem to believe that aborting our mission will help the SS's takeover. Our mission is scheduled to be completed on the twenty-second. Hilga and her parents have offered us their farm as a refuge until then. Because yesterday was quiet, we—that is, myself, Jacob, and Sergeant Schmidt—were able to get some rest. We thought we had escaped from Manz's people's observation. But apparently we haven't.

"In the middle of the night, Jacob was checking the trees behind the buildings when someone attacked him. Jacob was taken by surprise, but apparently he jerked away, and the blow, from a rod of some kind, hit his arm and he cried out. Fortunately the sergeant, who had the prior observation time period, was relieving himself behind some nearby trees. The assailant raised the rod, but Schmidt drew his pistol and fired. As the attacker fell with Schmidt's bullet in his chest, the descending rod, a steel two-foot-long billy club, hit Jacob's head with only a glancing blow. Although it wasn't a deadly hit, he fell to the ground, unconscious.

"When I heard the pistol's shot, I ran to the house's back door and cautiously opened it. With the moon at almost full, I saw the sergeant, with his weapon in his hand. I quickly joined him. We spent several minutes searching the immediate area for additional intruders. Not finding any, we carried Jacob into the house. Hilga and Wilhelmnina had been wakened by the sound of the shot. They quickly examined Jacob, administering first aid. Then Hilga called you.

"After putting your auto into the barn, the sergeant is continuing his surveillance of the area. I'm surprised that it was an SS man. Yes, it's the SS. Schmidt identified him as Lieutenant Colonel Brummeir, who is, or at least was, the head of Manz's unit in the SS. For some reason, he was wearing the uniform of a private. Why the attack? Perhaps he wanted to be a hero, getting us all by himself. He used the club for silence. In any case, we must go somewhere else until the day after tomorrow. If he found us, others will too, if they haven't already."

Hans held up his hand. "All right, I understand the present situation. But who are you? You were identified all those years ago by a fake Knights Cross."

Hilga spoke up. "Wilhelm and I have discussed this. He has no recollection about the medal—where it came from or why it was around his neck. You are aware of his amnesia problem. It began more than twenty years ago. We know him as a German soldier who has served his country and is doing so now. That Hoff man, Manz's and Heydrich's man, was looking for something to discredit the Abwehr, and apparently your story about the medal was sufficient to make Wilhelm and his current mission the target."

Lessing spoke out, "Yes, putting those together with what happened during Jacob's interrogation by Manz last month in Cherbourg and earlier this month in Brussels apparently has made Manz, Heydrich, and perhaps even Himmler highly suspicious of our mission. And I'm sure you know, Hans, that the SS's solution to a problem is often death."

By the time the sun was close to reaching its peak for the day, Hilga and Wilhelmnina had left for the hospital. Schmidt came in and reported that there didn't appear to be any more SS men. He had put the dead Brummeir in a shallow grave.

Hans had been quiet for several minutes. After the sergeant's report he spoke up. "Wilhelm, I believe I have done you bad harm. I told Hoff my doubts about the medal's authenticity. This may have been the reason for the SS's action. What can I do to help you complete your mission?"

Before Lessing could answer, Max came into the room and said that Hilga was on the phone and wanted to talk to the doctor. Hans followed him into the next room and picked up the telephone's receiver. "Yes?"

"Something strange has happened," Hilga said. "A few minutes ago, when Wilhelmnina had gone into the dining hall for a cup of coffee, she was approached by an SS sergeant named Hecker. He asked where Doctor Brachman was. She said she didn't know. Rather than leaving, he poured himself a cup of coffee and sat down beside her.

"He then began to try to hit on her. He bragged that he was in charge of the hunt for a traitor—actually two traitors: an Oberst and a British spy. He then asked her if she had seen any strangers in the area in the last day or so. She said no, and that she had to get back to a patient. She then came to me and is waiting here beside me to see what she should do next, if anything. She says she was quite nervous, and she thinks that perhaps this may have alerted Hecker that she knew more than she had told him. Hans, can you ask Wilhelm what we should do? Are we in danger? Frankly, even though I'm scared, I want to help them for two reasons. We are Germans, and we should do what we can to assist in our country's war efforts. And if doing this requires us to choose, it's the admiral over Himmler. Also, Wilhelm is our friend."

"You are right," Hans said. "Call me back in five minutes." He then walked back into the room and motioned to Lessing to be quiet.

After a couple of minutes, he said, "I've told Hilga that she and Wilhelmnina should continue working as if nothing out of the ordinary has happened. We have to get out from here at once, not only to help you complete your mission, but also to protect Hilga and her family. Have Schmidt drive my auto, the Mercedes, and follow me. I'll drive yours to a remote area that I know of and leave it. I'll then join you. I have a recommendation for where we can go. Heinrich Fuerst has a cabin—actually more like a castle—about ten kilometers from here. He may be there."

"He was going there when we talked to him in Freiburg the night before last," Lessing said as he went to the front door and outside and spoke to Schmidt.

As he returned to the house's front door, it was opened by Hans, who said, "Come on in and we will carry the lieutenant to the Mercedes. Then you follow me."

When Schmidt pulled up in the Mercedes convertible, Hans helped Lessing put the unconscious Jacob into the rear seat. Lessing then followed, sitting on the seat beside him. Hans got into the sedan that the three of them had been using and headed out the driveway. Schmidt, his automatic pistol on the seat beside him, followed him.

CHAPTER FORTY-SIX

SCHWARZWALD (BLACK FOREST),
GERMANY
JULY 20–22, 1940

About half an hour later, the two vehicles arrived at the entrance of the secluded site's driveway. Turning into it, they quickly disappeared from the road as the driveway curved into a grove of trees. A surprised Heinrich Fuerst, having heard the sound of a motor, was stepping out of the front door as the Mercedes pulled up. Hans Brachman, who was an old friend of Fuerst dating back to the First World War, appeared to have taken over the concealment process. He explained the need for concealment of the three Abwehr agents, apparently from Manz's SS, for the next two nights. On the morning of the second day, they would take his Mercedes and drive across the border into Switzerland and on to the noon meeting in Bern.

Schmidt parked the Mercedes behind the building. As he joined them inside, Fuerst was saying, "There is a bridge across the river into Switzerland near Stein. It's rather remote. Perhaps you could have your contact meet you there. It's less than an hour from here. I can contact Julian and have him arrange it."

"Sound like a good choice," Lessing replied. "And I'm not surprised that you can contact him. But be careful. Have him go through Oster."

Fuerst was the perfect host, and after several hours' rest, and a quiet day and two nights, they stepped out into a heavy summer downpour at dawn on July 22. Brachman and Lessing were in the rear seat of the Mercedes, with the now-conscious Jacob between them. Their host had contacted his son Julian, who had, through the general, contacted Juhol, who they thought was their double agent when in truth he was Britain's, was in Bern with James Bradford, and Julian let him know about the plan change.

CHAPTER FORTY-SEVEN

SCHWARZWALD (BLACK FOREST), GERMANY
JULY 21–22, 1940

Hecker was sure that Wilhelmnina was lying, but he had to be careful. She was a nurse caring for seriously wounded soldiers. All he did, using a hospital telephone, was inform Manz, who was in Freiburg, that the Abwehr team was somewhere in the area. And he had learned, by questioning other hospital personnel, that Dr. Brachman was not there.

Manz mulled over the situation. The twenty-second was the next day. The main characters were here in the Schwarzwald, near the Swiss border. Of course the new agent was on his way, probably to England. But why all the secrecy? If he succeeded, would it be a feather in Canaris's cap? And Brachman: how did he fit into the picture? Was he helping the trio? If so, how?

Should he inform Heydrich? He checked the time. Not quite noon. Less than a day. By the time he contacted Heydrich and got permission to do something, it would probably be too late to stop whatever it was that Lessing was up to. Whatever they were up to, he had to stop them. He would take care of the problem. He put through a telelpone call to his SS office in Berlin. He gave an order to Pacher. By three o'clock, Pacher had rounded up four SS soldiers and the five of them were airborne for the three-hour, 400-mile flight to Freiburg.

After his call to Pacher, Manz drove the twenty miles to Schonau, where he joined Hecker. While Manz went to the town's police station, Hecker arranged temporary quarters for the seven members of the SS.

Manz had the local police chief order all the police in the southern Schwarzwald to be on the alert for three men, probably dressed as soldiers. A thought came to him. "Does Dr. Brachman have a car?" he asked the chief. Brachman's black Mercedes convertible sedan became part of the search, as it was not at the hospital. It was pretty well known in the Schwarzwald.

CHAPTER FORTY-EIGHT

THE STEIN BRIDGE
JULY 22, 1940

There was no action for the rest of the day and night, until shortly before noon on July 22, when there was a telephone report that a black Mercedes with several men in it had been observed in the Stein area of the Schwarzwald. All morning there had been heavy summer rainfall, which increased to a downpour by noon. It was so intense that the observer, who was only several yards from the vehicle, could not count the number of people in it before it vanished from sight into the downpour.

Thirty minutes later, Manz was seated in the front cab of the SS truck with its driver, Hecker. With Pacher in the covered back of the truck were the four troopers from Manz's Berlin SS unit. The previous day, Hecker, thinking that the Stein bridge over the Rhine River into Switzerland might be the objective of the Abwehr group, had driven to the area around the bridge. He was able to get to the bridge through the rain. As the truck approached the bridge from the northwest, Hecker saw the black Mercedes emerging from the dense rainfall to the east.

Hecker, flooring the truck's accelerator, beat the black Mercedes in the race to the bridge's entrance. He glided to a stop, blocking the car's entry to the bridge and Switzerland.

As the Mercedes screeched to a stop, Hecker saw Brachman, Oberst Lessing, and Rosenstein, dressed as a civilian, in the backseat of the convertible sedan. Schmidt, the driver, was sitting alone in the front seat. Because of the rain, he had raised the convertible's canvas top.

Pacher, as the truck skidded to a halt, jumped out and ran through the rain to the right side of the truck's cab. Acting like he was kowtowing to a superior officer, he pulled open the door and held out his left arm as if to help Manz out of the cab. When Manz held out his right arm and stepped down to the truck's step, Pacher grabbed it, pulled the smaller Manz all the way out of the cab, and swung him around so that Manz's back was against his chest, his left arm around Manz's neck. With his right hand he pressed his Lugar pistol against the right side of Manz's head. He shouted to the SS troopers who had jumped out of the truck, "Stand back and drop your weapons or I'll kill him."

To Schmidt he shouted, "Swing around the truck and drive across the bridge."

To Brachman: "Get out and leave them, and stay on this side." Brachman didn't move.

"Now. Out," Pacher said. "Across the river, in Switzerland, they will be safe. Quick. Out."

Opening the car's door, Jacob jumped out, reached down, and grabbed the pistol from the seat beside Schmidt.

The four SS troopers seemed frozen with surprise when one of their kind acted as Pacher had. But when Jacob moved, so did they, raising their weapons, preparing to fire.

"Stop!" Pacher shouted.

When they didn't, he fired, Manz slumping and dropping to the ground as Pacher loosened his left-arm grip. Simultaneously he swung his right arm around and emptied the pistol at the four.

Simultaneously also, Jacob fired his weapon. The four dropped to the ground.

Hecker's arm appeared through the cab's door, aimed at Pacher. In the Mercedes, Lessing jerked his pistol out of its holster, swung up his arm, and fired, emptying the weapon. Hecker's arm dropped, as did his body, following his arm as it received the final bullets from the weapon.

Shouting to Jacob to get back into the car, which he did, Schmidt swung the car around the truck and entered the bridge.

Surprisingly, Manz was able to raise his right arm with his pistol in its hand. Aiming it at the rear of the car, he fired. A hole appeared in the back of the canvas top of the convertible.

This left only Abwehr soldier Pacher and military doctor Brachman alive, on Germany's side of the river.

The Abwehr sergeant Josef Schmidt then drove the Mercedes across the bridge with the fictitious Abwehr agent Rosenstein and his father, the Oberst Wilhelm/William Lessing, into Switzerland.

Stopping fifty yards or so from the end of the bridge, Schmidt looked around. There was no one there. No James Bradford or Juhol waiting.

Schmidt turned around and saw that Jacob was holding his father's limp body, which had blood running from a wound in his chest, his bruised left arm under him.

"What happened?" Schmidt asked.

"I don't know," Jacob said. "He just slumped down. Someone must have fired at the back of the car. He's bleeding from his chest, so the bullet must have passed clear through him."

"Here," Schmidt said. He picked up Brachman's bag off the floor of the vehicle, opened it, and, rummaging around inside, pulled out a roll of white bandage. Jacob ripped Lessing's officer's shirt off and wrapped a bandage several times around his body.

"We must get him to hospital. Where is my grandfather?" Jacob asked as he got out of the car into the dense rainfall. Schmidt did also. There was no one within the circle of visibility.

Looking at his watch, Schmidt said, "It's past the scheduled meeting time. And the Oberst must get to a hospital. Let's see. Wait," he said as Rosenstein started to speak. For the next few minutes the only sound was that of the pouring rain. Then Schmidt said, "Get in the car. Follow the road, and you will find someone who can direct you to a hospital. Listen," he said as Jacob again started to speak. "You have appropriate documents for Switzerland. I don't. Go. I'm going back to Germany."

"Wait!" Jacob shouted. "The Oberst doesn't either."

After visually searching the front and back seats, he went to the back of the Mercedes and opened the trunk. He reached in and pulled something out. Returning to the other two, he said, "Let's put these on him" and held out a pair of pants. They removed Lessing's military trousers, replacing them with Brachman's. With his bare upper body, he was no longer easily identified, as had largely been the case decades earlier.

"Okay," Schmidt said as he turned and disappeared into the dense rain.

As Rosenstein was sliding into the driver's seat, he slid his weapon under the front seat. He started the engine and headed south on the left side of the highway.

CHAPTER FORTY-NINE

SCHWARZWALD (BLACK FOREST), GERMANY

JULY 22, 1940

Schmidt ran back through the driving rain across the bridge to the truck, where Pacher and Hans, having pulled Manz's and Hecker's bodies over where those of the troopers lay, were sitting in the truck's cab out of the rain.

"Where's the Mercedes?" Pacher said, alarm in his voice.

"My Mercedes," Hans echoed.

"There was no one on the other side, and the Oberst has been wounded. The young soldier has appropriate Swiss papers, so I told him to head south and get his father to a hospital," Schmidt said.

"What do you mean, 'father'?" asked Hans.

"Yes. Father and son," Schmidt replied. "I have known ever since Brussels. I know people. Now let me think."

He walked fifty yards or so and looked around. All he saw was the dense rain falling on grass-covered, relatively flat ground.

He returned to the truck.

"Apparently no one knows what has happened here. The dense rain must have restricted sight and sound. Let me think."

Pacher and Brachman remained seated on the truck's step while Schmidt slowly walked around the truck in deep thought. When he got back to the two, he said, "We've got to get rid of these bodies. Come on. Let's dump them in the river. It's going into flood stage, so they should be carried quite a distance from here. Then we can drive the truck to where you put our vehicle, Hans."

By nightfall the bodies had disappeared and they had recovered the Abwehr vehicle, with which they had returned to Heinrich Fuerst's "cabin." They stayed there until the next day, July 23. After a quick breakfast, supplied by Fuerst, they drove north to Abwehr headquarters in Hamburg, dropping Brachman at the Schonau hospital, where he resumed his duties as a doctor.

In Hamburg, they gave their report to Majorgeneral Oster. It said the Abwehr's exchange with James Bradford had been completed, although they didn't know for certain that it had been, thereby completing the Abwehr's part in the agreement. But at a price. Oberst Wilhelm Lessing had been killed shortly after he had made his delivery of Rosenstein to Juhol and an unknown man on the Swiss side of the bridge over the Rhine River near Stein. After the delivery, there had been a skirmish with some unknown armed men, who shot the Oberst as he was crossing the bridge heading back to Germany. The shooters, who could have been members of the SS, were shot by Schmidt and Pacher. The body of the Oberst had fallen into the river.

On their way out of the Schwarzwald, they had reported the skirmish to the local police chief. Speaking for Admiral Canaris, the commander of the Abwehr, they suggested that he accept the story of armed unknowns near the bridge near Stein. They left the name of Hans Brachman out of the report.

As Pacher was the only member of the SS with whom Manz had communicated, and he was buried somewhere in the ranks of the Abwehr, there was no member of the SS left who could tell Heydrich what had happened to Manz, Hecker, Pacher, and the four SS troopers. There was only the burned-out truck in a field in the Schwarzwald near the Rhine River. The Freiburg office said that a Sergeant Hecker had requisitioned the use of Corporal Holtz and Private Brummeir. However, Holtz knew only that he had seen Brummeir riding off on a motorcycle following the three Abwehr men. The SS subunit in Berlin, having lost its top three men in a little over a week, was dissolved. Its remaining troopers were transferred to other units. And Heydrich was so deeply involved with his anti-Jewish program that his anti-Canaris sentiment was relegated to a back burner.

CHAPTER FIFTY

BLETCHLEY, ENGLAND

AUGUST 10, 1940

At five in the afternoon of August 10, Prime Minister Winston Churchill arrived at a military hospital near Bletchley Park. He was accompanied by Colonel Robertson. His secretary having phoned ahead, the P. M. was met by a nurse at the hospital's entrance. She escorted them to a private room on the second floor.

Opening the closed door, the nurse entered the room. There was a single bed, two chairs, and a small table. There was a closed door, presumably to a lavatory. Sitting in one of the chairs, facing the room's door, was a rather large man, dressed in a bathrobe and wearing slippers.

Entering the room first, she announced in a firm voice, "Colonel Lessing, the prime minister has arrived."

Lessing, who had been informed of the visit several hours earlier, with help from a nurse, had gotten out of the hospital bed and put on the bathrobe and slippers. He started to rise.

Churchill, stepping forward, said, "No, Colonel, sit down. If anyone should be rising in admiration for what you have done, it is me."

Seeing a look of bewilderment on Lessing's face, he continued. "The achievement of Fish Boat—it achieved everything we hoped it would. First, of course, was the deliverance of your son, Jacob.

"As to the other achievement, we have been advised by our sources in Germany that the fabricated defense plans that your father-in-law delivered to Admiral Canaris may have been the final bit of information that made the Germans abandon the Sealion invasion of our country. We will never know for certain, but it is quite possible.

"And I am glad that we didn't lose you. I understand that your son, Lieutenant Rosenstein, was instrumental in saving your life. The two of you are our country's heroes. I would like to hear your tale from you, however." He reached into a pocket and pulled out a watch. "I have an appointment at Bletchley Park, so I must say good-bye. Colonel Robertson will remain, as he has something to tell you." Stepping forward, he held out his hand to Lessing.

Lessing, who had been tongue-tied as the prime minister rambled on, held out his left arm. Seeing Churchill's questioning look, he said, "My wound has partially restricted the use of my right arm. Thank you, sir. Your comments are appreciated."

"Of course," Churchill said. He grasped Lessing's hand, gave it a couple of shakes, and turned around and headed toward the room's door.

"The successful completion of Fish Boat has fulfilled my entrance into the third phase of my life," Lessing said to the back of his country's leader as he exited through the door, followed by the nurse, who closed the door after them.

Robertston stepped forward and said, "Well, William, I talked to your doctor and he says you are well on the way to recovery. He believes the only lasting consequence will be slight restriction of your arm. How do you feel?"

"Not too badly. It could have been much worse, if Jacob had not acted as promptly as he did. The prime minister said you have something to tell me."

Robertston replied, "I want you to join me and the Committee of Twenty. You have worked with Johol. And your knowledge of the Abwehr operations will be most valuable. And on a personal note, while war is war and involves the killing of people to win, you won't be directly involved in such action with people on the other side whom you may know. The success of your work will shorten the war. The doctor says you should be able to get back to work in a couple of weeks or so. We will welcome you. But now, you said that Jacob may have saved your life. I have some time. Can you tell me what happened?"

"Of course. Have a seat," Lessing said, pointing at one of the chairs. "Let's have some coffee." He pushed a button on the wall beside the bed. Ten minutes later, after an orderly had brought in a pitcher of coffee and two mugs, Lessing began the tale that Jacob had told him on the second day after he had brought his father to a hospital in Basel, Switzerland.

Lessing began by telling about the action that had occurred just before and after the crossing of the bridge. Then he said that Schmidt had got some hunting pants out of the Mercedes trunk. "They took my uniform trousers off and put the pants on me. The waist was a bit larger than mine, but as I was lying down, it was no problem. They had torn my uniform shirt off when they had bandaged me. When the police questioned Jacob, he said apparently my identification papers were in my shirt pocket, which he had thrown away when he treated the wound.

"Schmidt then left, disappearing into the dense rain and apparently crossing the bridge back into Germany. With me lying down on the rear seat, Jacob drove up the road away from the bridge. Because he had driven only in Britain, he took off on the left side of the road! With the rain extremely limiting visibility, he didn't see the car heading toward him until the last minute. He saw that the left side of the road was clear, so he swung off the road to the left for a safe stop. Or so he thought. Unfortunately, the other driver also saw that the adjacent side of the road was clear, so he swung over too. Unfortunately, Jacob's safe left-side shoulder was also the other driver's safe right-side shoulder. Both drivers hit their brakes and pulled up safely a yard or so apart.

"Jacob probably heaved a sigh of relief when the passenger door of the other car opened and his grandfather James Bradford got out. Jacob wouldn't tell me how he did it, but within a couple of hours I was lying on a seat in a train on the way to a hospital in Basel. Five days later, I was on a plane heading for England. That's it."

Lessing finished. "Now tell me, other than to see how I'm doing, why are you here?"

Robertson took a sip of his coffee and said, "Continuing, you can't return to Canaris because, although he may not know who you really are, he probably knows by now that you aren't who he thought you were. And Heydrich's SS will be on the lookout for you. As far as they are concerned, you are dead. Wait," he said. "Let me finish. Schmidt is an amazing man. He contacted Johol, knowing he was a double agent, thinking that he was Germany's. He asked him to tell his handler in Britain that he had reported to Canaris that you had been killed. He did this, he said, because he wanted you to survive. And that going back to Germany would not be a good idea. Johol asked him why he was so concerned. He replied, 'Because he is the father of the woman I'm going to marry.'"

"Amazing, he is," said Lessing. "If he survives the war, I'll welcome him as my son-in-law. Now, let's get back to my situation. This committee: when will I start?"

"Well, the doctor says you should stay here for a few days. Let's say ten days from now—say, the twentieth. I'll send someone here in a couple of days, for an hour or so, to bring you up-to-date on our affairs."

"Thank you," said Colonel William Lessing—once known as Oberst Wilhelm Lessing.